Classic Sw

In the Tradition of Conan the Barbarian
The Mightiest Swordsman Who Ever Walked the Earth.

KYRIK
WARLOCK
WARRIOR

Book 1

by Gardner Francis Fox

Originally printed in 1975

digitally transcribed by Kurt Brugel 2017
for the Gardner Francis Fox Library LLC

Gardner Francis Fox (1911 to 1986) was a wordsmith. He originally was schooled as a lawyer. Rerouted by the depression, he joined the comic book industry in 1937. Writing and creating for the soon to be *DC comics*. Mr. Fox set out to create such iconic characters as the *Flash* and *Hawkman*. He is also known for inventing *Batman's* utility belt and the multi-verse concept.

At the same time, he was writing for comic books, he also contributed heavily to the paperback novel industry. Writing in all of the genres; westerns, historical romance, sword and sorcery, intergalactic adventures, even erotica.

The Gardner Francis Fox library is proud to be digitally transferring over 150 of Mr. Fox's paperback novels. We are proud to present - - -

Table of Contents:

Introduction

Chapter 1

Chapter 2

Chapter 3

Chapter 4

Chapter 5

Chapter 6

Chapter 7

Chapter 8

Introduction

In the old legends and the almost forgotten folklore of mankind, it is said by men who claim to know that there were other men on this our Earth of which no written record remains. These men, lost in the mists of Time though they are, yet remain our ancestors.

Wise men often speak of cycles of civilization, in which men and nations rise and fall into oblivion, of catastrophes from space which have devastated our planet, of ice ages, of fallen moons and other destructive influences that come and go, wiping out all evidence of those past eons. From time to time, slight traces of those past civilizations have been found by us, and are thought to be no more than an interesting, mysterious artifact which, embarrasses the scientists and the historians.

For those who doubt, I call attention to the Piri Reis maps, which use Cairo as a projection point and which show our world perfectly, as though mapped out from an aerial photograph by an airplane or a satellite. They show the continent of Antarctica as though it were not hidden by uncounted tons of snow and ice. Our own scientists have only discovered this continent's outlines very recently, by sonic probings beneath the ice. Piri Reis lived in the eighteenth century. He did not make them. From whence did he get them? Who took the aerial photographs from which those maps were made? As far as our written records go, it was not until this century that we had airplanes or satellites that could make such photographs.

Ancient records say man has been visited from space by other intelligent beings. Possibly mankind itself had space travel long and long ago. There is a plain called Nazca in Peru, which some say was a vast landing field for spaceships, with giant markers to show its direction to any spaceships entering our atmosphere. Men also say that the "terrace" at Baalbek is also a landing field for spaceships.

Examine also, if you will, the idol of Tiahuanaco, that shows the exact position of the stars as they were—27,000 years ago. According to our beliefs, there were only cavemen around at such a remote period in Time. Was that idol made by those members of an extinct Terran civilization that perished in some planet-wide war or other disaster?

There was a giant race of men who lived on Earth in the dim past.

They are mentioned in the Bible. They are mentioned also in Indian and native folklore that calls them "gods", that says they taught many things to the race of ordinary men who lived on Earth in those days.

I call your attention to the antique electric battery—nobody knows where it came from, but it is very old—now to be seen in the Baghdad museum. Plato spoke of a vast continent on the other side of the Atlantic Ocean. Plato lived some centuries before Christ, and Columbus did not discover America until the last few years of the fifteenth century. Where did Plato derive his knowledge of North and South America?

All these are but a smattering of mysteries we cannot answer. Yet they postulate the fact that at one time, there were other high civilizations upon the face of the Earth. They have no names, they leave no traces behind, or if they do, they are such traces that must remain forever inexplicable.

I suggest also that here and there on our world—in Death Valley, in the ruins of Khara Khota in the Gobi Desert—there are evidences of a titanic destructive power used to obliterate whatever was below it. An atom bomb out of the unknowable, far distant past? A bomb which helped, along with the glaciers of the ice ages, earthquakes, even the turning of the Earth upon its axis, which changed the then tropical regions into what we know today as the arctic and the antarctic, to bury out of sight the remains of mystical kingdoms and faraway lands. I think of Atlantis, a memory from those olden times, which was destroyed in a single day and a night. Were there many Atlantises blotted out by past cataclysms?

Atlantis is only a name for the forgotten memories of mankind. Perhaps Lemuria is such another name, and Gondwanaland, Masma, Pohjola, Aluminor, as well. Bolivian legends have it that there were very ancient civilizations, and that they were destroyed in a battle with a non-human race of beings. The animal-headed gods of ancient Egypt? Is the Biblical story of Michael battling the fallen angels a race memory of this encounter? There is no proof, it becomes only an exercise of the imagination.

Fulcanelli says alchemy is the link between those very old and now forgotten civilizations and our own. The Eskimos have legends that claim they were brought to the far north in flying machines. The Popul Vuh also tells us about a very ancient civilization, as do other writings no one pays any attention to, any more.

I think that there is truth where there is legend, as Schliemann proved at Troy. I think that there were other civilizations, long forgotten by mankind, that exist only in our myths.

It is of those other times and other lands I would write, of a barbaric period before the rise of a high civilization—perhaps the very one that took the photographs which served as a model for the Piri Reis maps. Their times were not as ours, they could work magic and wizardry, the art, now since lost, that gave certain members of their society the power of mind over matter.

Kyrik lived in that world. He was a warlock as well as a warrior, in that Time before the first Ice Age and while two moons were in the sky. Later one of those moons was to crumble and form a Saturnian ring to shut off sunlight and so bring that first Ice Age, but when Kyrik lived, that future was not known.

The seven seas may have been four in number, or ten, when he was wenching and looting, raising up kingdoms and toppling them. Even the shapes of the continents were not as ours, as suggested by the Continental Drift theory, and demonolotry and sorcery were living things, as science is today.

Kyrik was a king and a barbarian, as well as warlock and warrior. This is his story. Or at least, a beginning to it, for much is to be told of Kyrik and his world, of the men he fought and the women he loved, of the mysteries and wonders of the lands where he rode his black stallion, and wielded his sword, Bluefang. You will find mention also of Illis, that lovely demon-goddess whom he loved and worshiped, and who took a very personal interest in his affairs.

It happened a very long time ago, in a world that has been forgotten. And now to Kyrik—of the Victories.

Gardner F. Fox

Chapter 1

Aryalla the sorceress walked the streets of the bazaar, hunting for that which had no name, which might not even exist. She felt inside her that she would know that which her black eyes hunted, when she touched those eyes to it.

Yet she might be wrong.

Has a legend any shape?

The street vendors hawked their wares, a flashing carpet from Thakispan made a potpourri of color where a dark-faced man waved it; a bronze vase enameled by a craftsman of Ivareen caught the rays of the dying sun and sparkled; a curving sword from the distant southlands was displayed beside a shield in which rare gems glimmered. Yet she had eyes for none of these.

She walked with firm steps, her feet bare in black sandals that matched the ebon of her cloak. Her long black hair fell free, like that of a harlot from the traveling fairs, but it was banded by silver links; and her face, aristocratic and touched by the refinement of royal blood, was cold and almost lifeless. Only her fine eyes lived, stabbing at a copper pot or a set of carved warriors with which to play the game called oganal.

Long had she walked the avenues and the bazaars of her world, from the frozen barrens of Isthulia to the sun-baked deserts of Arazalla, shivering in one clime and cooking in another, drawing her strength from the hate and the need for vengeance that ran with her blood in her veins. From time to time she had used the thin poniard hanging at her belt to defend her life; she had offered gifts at strange altars to even stranger gods, that her quest might find an ending. Yet with every step her spirit lagged and her head hung a little lower.

"So long. It has been so long," she whispered into the hood of her dark cloak. "Almost I begin to think that the legend is a false one."

What is a legend? A whispered word in the night, a tale spun by a storyteller in a bazaar, a hint of something long desired and put into words for another to hear. Men said Kyrik lived, men said the spell was still potent. Somewhere in the world he knew a life that was also a death, but that he waited. Waited, hoping. Waited

"I shall find him," she snarled between red lips, making a fist of her right hand. "I shall. No matter how long it takes me."

Aryalla had conjured up demons to aid her, yet the demons had been powerless in the face of that ancient necromancy that had doomed Kyrik. They had told her so, regretfully, in the darkest hours of the night, whispering that they might not be heard except by her own ears. Kilthin, Abakkan, Rogrod, their names were many, their powers vast. Yet they could not help her.

A horseman in the gray and silver of the rulers of Pthesk went by her at a gallop, a hoof splattering her feet with slops. She shrank back into shadows, muttering against the filth staining her flesh.

Yet she had endured worse than this, and would endure even more, if need be. She must find Kyrik! There was a desperate need in her to look upon his face, to listen to his voice. Aye! As great a need as he himself must feel, if legend spoke truth.

Her feet carried her from one end of the bazaar to the other, and she turned back, despair rounding her shoulders. Her belly ached, it had been a full day since she had eaten, but she cared naught for that. She would feed through her eyes, could she but behold that which she sought, that which she would know upon first sighting, though it had no name, though it was unknown. Her nostrils pinched at their corners, her eyes sunken slightly in her lovely face, she searched on.

Her feet took her into shop after shop, stall after stall. She was offered the silver lamps of Karalon, and the golden bells of Amanoy, raiment of rare workmanship from the looms of Inisfall. To each of these she shook her head and the shopkeepers, the sellers of wares, could sense her despair that was close to tears.

"What is it you seek, mistress?" they would ask. "I shall know it, I shall!" They looked upon her and their eyes knew sympathy, for she was a shapely woman and lovely, and they thought she would be better off in a bed with a strong man than wearing out her feet and those thin black sandals hunting something to which she could not put a name. Always, she walked on.

The sun was setting when she came at last to a little shop at the very end of the bazaar. Its proprietor was a tiny man, very thin and very old, with eyes rheumy from near blindness, and he fussed over a chest that was beyond his power to move.

The sorceress watched him a moment, eyes misting with pity, and then she went to help him, putting her white hands with the red fingernails to a corner of the chest and shoving. When the coffer was tight against the wall of the shop, the old man bobbed his head in gratitude.

"My thanks, gracious lady. I am an old man, I have lived too many years. It is not right that I must earn my bread in such a fashion."

"All life is a problem, old one," she smiled. "That thrice—cursed boy I hired has gone off with a girl."

"Youth calls to youth."

"Leaving me with this old thing from Tantagol. It is very heavy, I haven't even examined it. I'll wait until the morrow."

The woman stared at him, scarcely breathing. "From Tantagol? You say—it comes from Tantagol?"

The old man chuckled, nodding. "Aye, from that land where Devadonides rules. Devadonides the Accursed, the Cruel, the Unfeeling. Magician and king in one! I went through Tantagol very swiftly, lady, I had no wish to linger, though my trade was brisk. I sold and I bought, I bartered as I have not done for a long time, until the guards came and assaulted me, and made me pack my goods in the middle of the night, and leave."

"From Tantagol," she whispered, and stared at the chest with wide eyes. "You say you have not looked inside it? And this chest holds those things you bought and bartered for in those lands of Devadonides?"

His voice sharpened. "Might you be interested in goods from Tantagol? If so, I will show them to you on the morrow when my lad returns, having gotten his bellyful of girl-flesh. But for now, I am an old man. I am tired. I would close my stall and eat, and sleep. Ah, sleep."

"No," said Aryalla. "I will look now." The old man gasped. "It is dark, almost."

"Then light a lamp. Fah! I'll pay you for the oil. But I must see, I must."

She sank on her knees beside the chest and ran palms over it as if it were the skin of a lover. The chest was old, black with centuries, and its iron hasps were rusted. Yet the coffer was from Tantagol, and it had been in Tantagol that Kyrik...

"Open it!" she cried imperiously. "Yes, lady—yes. But let me light this lamp first, since you pay for its oil. I can barely see in the dark, but with a light, I'll better be able to show you what I brought from Devadonides' lands."

"No need," she panted, her hands on the lid of the chest, pushing it up. Shadows lay long and black along the chest and in it, where daggers nestled beside folds of cloth, was here and there a bit of jewelry.

Her hands went into the chest, in among the bits of cloth and metal and gems, and her fingers searched like blind mice in the darkness. Then the lamp was overhead and the old man held it so she could see to lift out and examine that which might most please her.

A wind came down the avenues of the sellers; in it was the tang of rare perfumes out of Arazalla and spices from Parthanor. It ruffled the black cloak where the woman knelt, and stirred the rough brown homespun which the old man wore. It made the lamp-flame flicker so that shadows danced on the chest and its contents.

Aryalla gave a faint cry. Her fingers tightened about a length of cotton that held something hard sheathed inside it. Her hands felt of that object, went over it wonderingly while her heart slammed and thudded and her breath came swift and short in her throat.

"This is it," she whispered, even now scarcely believing.

She brought out the cotton and unrolled it. A six inch tall statue of a man carved out of solid bronze was in her cupped hands. There was paint on the statue, possibly enamel, it showed long yellow hair carved as if blowing free to an ocean breeze and a black and yellow fur kaunake about chest and shoulders, covering a shirt of chain-mail

"This shall I buy, old man," she declared. Her eyes could not leave the thing, it was so real. A sword hung in a tiny scabbard beside the broad leather belt studded with bronze bosses, there was a dagger on its other side. The face was dark with much sunlight, and the eyes of the statue were green.

"It is very valuable," he quavered. "It was sold to me by an old woman who discovered it in an attic of her home under a bit of broken planking. No telling how long it lay there. Years, probably. It's the work of a master hand, you can see that."

"A silver rhodanthe," she said. "A golden griff," he argued. She turned her head to look up at him and the old man cried out at what he saw written in her face and glowing in her eyes. Step by step he backed away from her until his buttocks wedged in a bolt of Inisfalian velvet, somewhat worn.

"Take it, as my gift," he quavered. The fury went out of Aryalla and she smiled, shaking her head. "Nay, now. You're right. This is worth good money. I've traveled great distances to put eyes to it and—shall I dishonor my search by niggardliness? Ten griffs, old one. Ten golden griffs, I give."

The old man shook as she rose to her feet. "Ten griffs?" he whispered.

"Aye, ten! What are ten griffs against what I seek?"

She counted them out into his palm, making a clinking sound with each coin, while he stared down at this new—found wealth with eyes that disbelieved. Beads of sweat came out on his forehead and now that he was rich, he must lift his head suddenly and look up and down the street, fearing robbery.

When she was done, the lady tucked the statue in its cotton batting inside her cloak, very tenderly. The old man licked his thin lips.

"Lady, answer me a question, I beg!"

"What question, then?"

"What's so valuable about that statue?"

"I've bought a legend this night, old man. And the name of the legend is—Kyrik!"

"Kyrik? Kyrik has been dead ten centuries"

"Say you so, old man? Then—he shall live again." The old man shrank back further against the velvet of Inisfall. "You're mad, lady. As my name is Prenn, you're witless. Kyrik died a thousand years ago. And you say he shall live again?"

"So goes the legend. And with my gold I've bought a legend, as I told you."

She brushed past him, stepped out onto the street. It was dark now, the two moons of this planet circled lazily overhead, beaming silver radiance down onto the bazaar, onto the white brickwork of the houses and the spires of this trade city of Joralegon. Hands clasped about the statue, she moved swiftly, walking purposefully and without her former tiredness, through the night with an occasional stab of lamplight from a shop or stall where men sorted out their wares or haggled with latecomers over prices.

Her heart sang within herself. She had known. As soon as her hands had gone around the statue, she had been aware that her quest was at an end. One part of the legend had come true. The statue was hers, and now she would make it live and carry out the balance of the prophecy.

Her sandaled feet took her into a quiet neighborhood, where little stone houses showed oil lamps at their narrow windows and roof eaves leaned above narrow streets. There were walled gardens to these houses, and here and there a tavern where wayfarers might quench their thirsts and put up for the night in a feather-bed

On silent feet she entered a tall house and crept up a narrow stairway lighted only by an oil cresset, the rustle of her cloak making the only sound around her. To the top floor of the building she went, and removing a large key from her leathern girdle-bag, inserted it into the lock of a narrow, tiny door. The door swung inward on oiled hinges.

The woman removed a tinder box from a tabletop, struck steel to flint and blew upon the spark as it fell on the tinder. A tiny flame glowed. She touched lamp-wick to flame and now the room could be seen in the bright flare of that lamp, to be wide and generous, sparsely fitted out with regard to furniture. There was only a table and a small chair, though there were many chests; and on the floor, which was bare wood, could be seen drawn in chalks of varying colors the great pentagram and then, a smaller one.

Aryalla sighed, let her cloak slip to the floor. Breathing fitfully, she ran to the smaller pentagram, put it standing in the center. She knelt a moment, studying the sturdy bronze figure, nodding to herself. Then she was up and moving, crossing to lift a worn wooden casket with tarnished silver fittings, putting it inside the great pentagram and throwing back the lid. Then she glanced about the room, sprang to the windows and drew the thick cloth drapes so that none might see into this garret chamber, so that no light might escape from it.

She stood then, loosed the clasp of her cloak, let it slip to the floor, revealing a shapely body clad in a tattered gown of Inisfalian silk that showed the flesh tints of her otherwise naked body beneath it. She was younger in the lamp light than she had seemed on the street, her black hair was thick and glossy, held by Karalonian silver pins and chains. Her cheeks were flushed, her black eyes glittered triumphantly.

A moment she paused, glancing about the room. Then her hand loosened clasps, the garment fell away and she stood proudly nude in the lamp-flames! Drawing air into her lungs, she then stepped into the center of the pentagram.

From the casket with the silver clasps she drew powders, rare and tinted with the hues of the rainbow, and of these she made piles, here and there, and touched them with the flame from the lamp-wick A blaze of colors lifted like pillars from the pentagram, went upward toward the beamed ceiling, hid amid the shadows.

A faint perfume came into the room. She raised bare arms.

"Demons of the worlds beyond our ken! You who dwell where no man's eyes may see, where no man's limbs may go except that it be your will—heed me Open wide your senses, hear my words!"

Aryalla paused to draw breath. "Kilthin of the frozen weald of Arathissthia. Rogrod of the red fire—lands of Kule! Abakkan the ancient, bent with the wisdoms of ten thousand times ten thousand nether worlds. I appeal, I cry out my needs, I summon you to this plane, this land, where I wait your coming."

There was a silence, aching to the ears. A coldness breathed across the room. Hoarfrost glimmered on tabletop and metal torches in the walls. The wooden paneling itself grew white with rime. And a voice that crackled with the icy weight of a hundred glaciers spoke in the air.

"Kilthin hears! Kilthin comes!" Heat swept like a blast off the southern deserts, baking, drawing the water from human skin. Gone were the rime glitters, except where a frostiness hung in the air beyond the pentagram. Now a red haze of heat lay between the floor and beamed ceiling and it breathed and its breath was that of living fire.

"I come," said a voice in which the beating and the roaring of hot flames lay hidden. "I listen, Aryalla of the ebon hai!"

Even as that whisper floated through the chamber, a leathery rustle was heard and a darkness came, shot with brownish gleamings, where something—crouched low to the floor and two baleful green eyes glittered.

"You called, Aryalla. I am here." Two tears crept down the cheeks of the girl who stood naked inside the great pentagram. She shivered slightly, then forced a smile to her full mouth.

"You have my thanks. I have been abandoned by all save you three old-friends. Once each of you said that not alone could I overthrow wicked Devadonides. I would need help from a legend. These were your words."

"I remember," whispered a leathery voice. "Aye, as do I," said the hoarfrost. Aryalla smiled. "And so I went in search of that legend named Kyrik, that warrior who was a warlock and lived a thousand years ago and was made into a statue by a wicked spell—or so goes the legend. I found that statuette this night.

"Behold—Kyrik!" Three breaths gusted in the chamber. Eyes—and that which passed for eyes—glinted where the lamplight caught them. The woman stirred, head turning as she scanned each feature, each movement, of these demons. The seconds passed, and a glow came about the tiny statuette so that it seemed there was a brilliance inside the bronze.

A hard voice whispered: "Who are you who touch Kyrik?"

The glow faded. Abakkon chuckled. "It's Kyrik, all right. Still the hard-nosed adventurer, king of Tantagol though he was. Many's the time I've come to his call, to help him out of one bit of trouble or another."

Aryalla clasped her hands between her breasts. "Can he aid me? Can he?"

Kilthin rasped icy laughter in which were the sounds of great bergs meeting and crunching together in the northernmost seas. "Aye, tis Kyrik, damn his eyes!"

"Why do you say that?" asked the woman, worried.

"Because he's a hard, proud man. A wencher of sorts, I remember. Beware of him, little sister of the pentagram. He'll have you on a bed, as soon as look at you."

"And what's so wrong with that?" asked fiery Rogrod. "Kyrik's still little more than a youth, for all his—age. And our daughter is very fair, eh?"

Aryalla flushed and attempted to hide her nudity from those demon eyes that searched it. But she was a beautiful woman, she knew it and gloried in it, and perhaps it was pride in that loveliness that made her stand so straight, so unashamed.

"Will he help me?" she asked softly.

"Who can answer that but—Kyrik?" Aryalla bent a little, craning toward the iciness, the heat, the leathery darkness on the floor. "Will you help me raise him? Will you cast off that bronze sheathing from his spirit, that prison which shackles the very soul of him?"

They agreed softly, in the black shadows where they hid.

And now the sorceress knelt, mixed other powders, red with yellow and blue with green, until she had other piles to set afire. And all this while, under her breath, she chanted words of a language that had been old when the reptilian people of Karsatheen had dug their first burrows.

The words went into the darkness lighted only dimly by the single oil lamp, and though Aryalla stumbled over their pronunciations now and again, there came a pale greenness into that darkness, flecked with vivid bolts of necromantic power.

And now the sorceress flung high her bare arms, chanted ever louder, so that those green beams glittered and hissed as though in torment, yet coalescing always into a ball of lightnings that danced upon the air currents. It hung there, quivering, denying itself to the service of the woman; as if it were alive, sparkling and scintillant with anger, with rebellion.

And now the leathery thing stirred. "Obey the command!" said Abakkon. "Aye—obey," breathed Rogrod. "You have no choice," whispered cold Kilthin. The green ball fell lower, lower. It hovered above the statuette, still raging, its whispers of hate for mankind and its service to them a gnawing in its vitals. It danced in the air over the bronze carving.

"Cantha fthnagen! Absothoth fertith!" cried Aryalla.

With a sigh the green ball dropped, enveloped the statuette.

"By the gods!" a bull voice roared. The greenness grew, bloated. It still hissed and sizzled, but now that hissing and that sizzling was muted, as though the ball muttered only. Inside as it swelled, a man could be seen; the statue expanding outward swiftly, growing upward. Still the verdant globe clung to that manlike thing, filling its flesh and pores, its veins and neurons, with the life it had sapped from it a thousand years before. "He lives," breathed the greenness. "Then begone," cried Aryalla. The globe faded. A man stood before the sorceress, giant in stature, his bronzed flesh rippling with massive muscles, his tawny hair long uncut, yet lending his craggily handsome face a hint of savage animality. The lamplight touched the plates of his mail habergeon, glinted on the buckle of his sword-belt, on the hilt of the great blade in its scabbard by his side.

His green eyes touched the woman, ran over her nakedness. A smile came upon his lips and grew. "By Illis and her brood! You are a woman!"

For the second time, Aryalla knew modesty. Those green eyes that searched her body were those of a wencher, of a king long used to the sensuous caresses of many women. Yet he did not move toward her, he let his eyes speak, and then he placed a big hand on his left arm, rubbed and massaged the flesh.

"I've been a long time without moving," he growled. "My flesh was turned to bronze, my insides to metal. It takes a while to—learn the art of moving."

The green—eyes saw Abakkon, a leatheriness crouching in the darkness, wings folded about its shoulders. The eyes widened. His head turned slowly, as though it ached, and now he saw the redness of Rogrod, the icy pallidity of Kilthin.

Kyrik nodded. "My thanks to all of you." He raised his arms, let the muscles bulge. He shook himself as might a great bear awakening from a long winter hibernation. Under the mail jacket, the habergeon, he wore a quilted gambeson. A black and yellow kilt of tiger fur encased his loins and a broad leather belt held sword and dagger scabbards. On his feet he wore short leather war-boots, with tiger-skin trimmings at their tops.

He stepped forward, moved out of the pentagram. Never did he take his eyes from the naked sorceress, it was as if she were the only living thing in the world. Before her he stood, brawny arms folded. "Now tell me why," he rumbled, with a smile upon his mouth. "There was a reason why you hunted down Kyrik of the Victories, why you sought to bring him back to life and—did so."

Her head went back, her pride answering his own. "Aye, there was a reason. I—hate. I would have you slay for me!"

"What man would you have die by Kyrik's hand?"

"Devadonides!"

Kyrik started, scowling. "Lives the devil yet? I thought by this time he would be dust in his coffin. Devadonides!"

"Aye, you know the forefather. Not his—descendant."

"And does the descendant still rule from the throne where I once sat? In Tantagol? Yes, yes. I see it in your eyes. So then, we are partners. And yet—I sense a disturbance in you, a worry."

"You are something more than I bargained for," the sorceress whispered. She could not control a human animal such as this, a giant of a man who towered above others of his kind, with a savagery in his eyes.

Perhaps he saw this in her face, for he rumbled laughter. "Na, na. I'm not the barbarian your eyes make me out to be. I have a sentiment in me of gratitude. And because of this, until I kill Devadonides for you, I am your servant."

She gave him a dubious look out of her faintly slanted eyes.

And then a voice cut across her own. "She has good cause to worry, Kyrik—and you have, as well."

The big barbarian swung about, stared at the leathery thing. "Abakkon. What croaking of danger is this I hear?"

"Devadonides is well served by sorcerers as able as the woman. Even now, those wizards sense your life. They run with warnings to King Devadonides. Soon a band of strong warriors will be setting out to slay you both."

Kyrik laughed. "By all the gods of Tantagol! It's good to be alive again, to know men hunt me with cold steel. Aye, by Illis I find a need in me for a good fight, after being a statue for so long."

His eyes touched Aryalla, ran lightly over her thrusting breasts. A fire came to life in his green eyes. "It's good to look upon a woman again, too! By Illis of the sterile caresses, it is. Na, na, girl. Don't cover yourself up. Indulge a man who's been cold metal for a thousand years."

"Best you leave this place," breathed a coldness. "Those wizards of Tantagol can find you easily enough by the traces of the potent magicks Aryalla had to work to bring you back to life."

Kyrik nodded. He moved to her fallen garment, lifted it and tossed it to the woman. She slithered her nakedness inside its worn thinness. Kyrik raised the cloak, held it for her.

"So no other eyes but mine can see how lovely you really are," he grinned, and kissed her soft throat.

"You have no time for wantonness," said the red thing known as Rogrod. "They come, these men of Devadonides, mounted on swift horses. They will be here before morning."

"And then they will slay you both," rasped Abakkon.

Kyrik growled, but nodded. His hand went to his sword, lifted it and let it fall back inside the scabbard. Aryalla was kneeling, gathering up the vials of powder, replacing them in the little coffer with the worn silver hasps. Kyrik moved toward her, sensing that Kilthin, Abakkon and Rogrod were disappearing into emptiness behind him.

"What else do you have to carry?" he asked. "Only this," she murmured, raising the coffer to show him.

His huge hand lifted her, brought her with him toward the door. Together, they went out into the black midnight hours.

Chapter 2

The streets were empty at this late hour. Only distantly could they hear the voices of revelers, drunken men and women frequenting the ale taverns and the wine-shops in this lower corner of the city. The air was fragrant with salt from the sea that rolled its waves in among the piles and seawalls of the waterfront. Their feet made hollow echoes on the cobbles of the streets as Aryalla guided the big man toward those faintly lighted taverns.

"I would eat," she explained. "I have not fed all day, and it has been a long one."

Kyrik chuckled thickly. "Ah, to eat. To drink I have not washed my throat with midland ale for the space of a thousand years, woman. Nor have I tasted the wines of Karanya, or bitten into a steak or the meats and vegetables of a stew." He drew his hand across his lips. "I drool at the thought. But—have you money?"

She smiled, "More than enough."

Always his eyes moved from house-front to eaves, upward toward the sky where the twin moons of Terra circled lazily. He scanned the darker shadows, watched where sleeping beggar lay, or drunk man staggered. It was, she thought, as though he were drawing sight and sound inside himself as a thirsting man swallows cool water on the desert sands.

"You love life," she whispered once. "More than you can know. Gods. To be imprisoned for ten times a hundred years inside cold metal, in darkness, living and yet not living. Illis of the soft breasts. It's like coming back from the grave."

They came to the street of wine-shops and ale taverns and now they smelled the cooking foods, the grape odors of spilled wines. Kyrik licked his lips, hastened his steps, his hand under her elbow keeping her at a half run.

"What of the soldiers seeking us?" she asked. "Pah! When Kyrik hungers, Kyrik eats. None shall stop us. Besides, would you have me fight on an empty belly?"

He needed food, if he were to fight. She could understand this, and so she tugged at him to enter the nearest of the many inns and taverns that abounded in the lower town. Yet he pulled back, he seemed always to be searching, searching.

At length, beneath a wooden sign in the shape of a bear, Kyrik halted, held the woman motionless. His eyes touched the sign, creaking lazily on a rusting chain where the waterfront breezes swayed it.

"Long ago, in my other life, there was a basilisk on chains like those. This is an old tavern, woman. Very old! I remember the way it used to be. It will not be a strange place to my eyes, and this I like."

He looked down at her, smiled. "Since I live again, I find I love life even more than I did—long ago. Mead will taste better, so will wine. And the kisses of a mouth such as yours. . ."

"I didn't bring you back to make love to me!"

"Na, na. Don't be angry. Yet—can you blame me?"

Aryalla searched his green eyes, found them hot with lust. I must remember, he has slept for a thousand years! I must be patient with his animal nature. Yet she admitted to herself that there was an attractiveness about him, he might make a good bedfellow. She shook her head slowly.

"No, I don't blame you. But you have more important things to do than think about a woman."

"Then let's get to it," he growled and pushed open the tavern door.

They walked into heat and half a hundred tables where men and women sat, watching a naked woman on a wine-wet tabletop. Fists and leather jacks pounded the tables in accompaniment to the stringed instruments of the musicians crouched in an alcove.

"Illis," breathed Kyrik, sniffing old, familiar smells.

His eyes were on the woman, devouring the large breasts and shimmying thighs. Aryalla felt jealousy bite within her. This giant was a man of primal emotions; she felt that in the old days he might have gone up to the woman and dragged her off the table and into a room where he might have her in privacy and at his leisure. Her tongue touched her lips.

Then he was half carrying her toward an empty table and gesturing a maidservant to attend them.

Aryalla he plumped down on a bench, sat beside her.

"Wine, first," he told the girl. "Chilled Kalerian. And stew. And bring a steak off the coals after that, with greens mixed together in a bowl with condiments."

The girl frowned. "Kalerian? We have no wine such as that. We have—"

"Bring it," Kyrik laughed. "And cold mead, as well. I've a thirst, I find."

He rested his elbows on the table and stared at the dancer. Aryalla feeling abandoned, shrank slightly within her cloak. Had she raised some sort of devil-man who would think more of his belly and his lusts than he would of vengeance? She had counted on his pride, his need for revenge. From what she had been able to learn of Kyrik from dusty old scrolls, he was a warrior who would not let another take that which was his own.

She stirred, put a hand to his hairy arm. "Remember, Devadonides sends soldiers." Without looking away from the naked woman who was bending backwards with her pale thighs spread far apart, he said, "I know. I want them to come, to find us."

"But to sit here. . ."

"Do you think Kyrik does not remember? Be assured I do, also that there is a want inside me. I must let the soldiers come to us, I won't waste time hunting for them."

"Hunting for them?" she gasped, appalled. "It's better if we flee from them, that we hide."

Now he turned his head and she shuddered at what she read in his green eyes. "Kyrik runs from no man. He who seeks out Kyrik with steel in his hand must face Kyrik's steel." His hand fell almost with affection on the hilt of his great sword. "As there is a need in Kyrik, so there is a need in Bluefang his blade. Bluefang is thirsty for the blood of Kyrik's enemies. It has been a thousand years since Bluefang drank."

What sort of monster had she raised from the dead? Aryalla shrank even deeper into her shrouding cloak. Her hand shook as she rested it on the tabletop. Instantly his huge paw covered it, squeezed. She felt the strength of his grip, though he did not exert his muscles. It was comforting, in a way, and she realized that it was Kyrik who was the leader, not she. He had taken over the role as easily, as naturally, as he wore his habergeon. In a way, Aryalla thought dazedly, she seemed no more than a child beside him.

The maidservant came with the chilled wine. Kyrik poured some into a leather beaker, shoved it toward her. His own jack he filled to the brim and lifted it to his lips. The woman watched him, half in awe. When he took away the beaker from his mouth, only the lees were left. He refilled the tankard.

Now other servants were bringing bowls of stew and bread still hot from the brick ovens, and wooden platters with steaks coal-grilled on them. The barbarian drew his dagger, slashed at the steak, stuffed a big chunk inside his mouth. He chewed, eyes half closed.

Then he lifted the wooden spoon, dipped it into the stew. Though she was hungry herself, the sorceress watched him in awe as he ate. Well, he hasn't tasted anything like that for ten centuries, she thought; it was enough to excuse him. She dipped a spoon into her own bowl.

When they were done, Kyrik sat back, grinning faintly.

"One more thing remains," he growled under his breath.

"And what's that?"

"There's a room upstairs, or used to be. Long ago I left a certain—something—inside it."

Aryalla widened her eyes. "After a thousand years, do you think it's still there?"

"I do. It was well hidden beneath a floor board, sorceress."

Two naked women were now writhing, twisting together upon the tabletop. A hushed audience watched them. One of the women was the dancer, the other had risen from among the watchers to join her. Almost regretfully, Kyrik took his eyes from their nudity, rose from the bench. The sorceress fumbled at her girdle, tossed down coins.

Then Aryalla went like a black shadow in her cloak, at his side. Through a hanging curtain they passed, in a narrow hall that ran almost the length of the old house. Kyrik paused, they could hear rats scurrying between the walls.

"Up yonder is a door," he breathed. They went softly, without sound, through that door and up a walled staircase to the upper story.

The barbarian counted doors, paused at the fifth one from the hidden staircase. His hand turned the brass knob, slowly.

The room was dark. Kyrik pushed her inside, came to stand beside her. They waited until their eyes grew used to the dark. Through the grimy windows a gleam of moonlight splashed silver on the floor. It was enough to see by, Aryalla knew. Her eyes touched the room, finding it empty save for an unmade bed, a cracked chair and a table with a pitcher and a washbasin on it.

Kyrik moved catlike across the room toward the farther wall. He knelt down, fumbled a moment at a floorboard. The wide wooden length came upward and his hand went out of sight. An instant later it reappeared with something wrapped in shrouding red linen that molded and fell apart to his touch. Kyrik opened his palm. A red jewel lay there, glinting in the moonlight.

The sorceress caught her breath, took a step, than two. She bent, eyes wide to take in the sheer size, the brilliance of that jewel.

"What is it?" she breathed. "It must be worth a fortune!"

He chuckled. "Men have named it the Pleasure of the World, or the Red Daughter of Desire. Take your choice. My own name for it is the Lust-stone! Here Gaze into it, woman."

She looked, her full red lips fell apart. Deep in those red deeps, a flame glowed. It leaped and danced as though to evil, unheard music. It was the shape of a naked woman, then a naked man, yet ever it danced on, to become a mere tongue of light that quested, pleaded, sought freedom from the facets of the gem.

And as she stared, Aryalla felt her blood pound hotter, knew the disturbing slamming of her heart, was aware that her breath came quicker, that her nipples grew rigid in desire. Yet still she could not look away, could not draw her eyes from that red temptation.

Big fingers closed about the ruby, hid it. The sorceress shook herself, the aftermath of passion still inside her flesh. Almost fearfully, she stared at the barbarian. "What is it? Where did you get that thing? With it. . ."

"Aye. With it, I can have any woman who stares into its depths." He waited a moment, then barked, "Can't I?"

She nodded silently, could not help risking a swift glance at the unmade bed. She wanted this big giant to throw her down on that rumpled mattress, to tear the clothes off her body, to possess her. Her breasts rose and fell. There was no need to tell him of her heat.

He laughed almost tenderly. "A rare thing, this. Once it belonged to Illis of the sterile kisses. It was made in some demon hell and given to an ancestor of mine who worshiped Illis, as I did. Illis—wants it back. She says—said—it was too powerful for a man to own."

"It is. Just the same. . . " Do you want to look into it a second time?" She almost nodded, she could not help it, the appeal of the red jewel was as wine to a toss-pot, as food to a starving man. She fought to quell the risings and falling of her breasts, the quiver of her thighs. A woman with lesser will power than hers would happily be a slave to the man who carried that jewel.

Then, out of the jealousy in her heart, she asked, "How do you intend to use it? Just to get yourself a bedfellow for a few hours pleasure?"

"Na, na. I have a greater need than that."

"What need?"

"You'll learn, in time." He replaced the loose plank, fitted it carefully into place. As carefully, he gathered up the loose bits of dust that were all that remained of the linen cloth that had shrouded the jewel, slipped them into the leather purse at his sword-belt.

"I leave no traces behind me, you'll notice," he grinned.

His huge hands placed the jewel in his almoner, wrapped about with a kerchief. Time had not aged his body nor the things upon it, that had been turned into necromantic metal when the spell had been laid upon him. Then he gripped Aryalla, hurried her out of the little chamber into the hell.

"We'll need horses."

"There are stables open at all hours of the night." They went swiftly from the upper hallway, down the walled staircase and through the tavern common room. Dawn was in the sky as they came out upon the cobbled street, splashing a pearly tint to the eastward where the lands of Tantagol and Ivareen lay, just waking. They hurried along the street, Aryalla half running to keep pace with his long legs.

At the stables, where a sleepy boy came running at their call, the sorceress handed over a golden griff and the boy returned with a big black stallion and a bay mare. They mounted up into worn but serviceable saddles and walked the horses along the streets. Kyrik rode easily in the saddle, as though long used to it. His head turned left and right, his eyes scanned the mean little houses past which they moved. The woman watched him slyly, her lips curving in a smile.

She said suddenly, watching his deep chest lift as he breathed in the salt air, "You seem like a man who never saw a building, never smelled stale fish and the tangy stinks of a waterfront."

"I haven't—for a thousand years. Can you understand my eagerness? I was dead for ten centuries, woman. I'm like a newborn babe."

"Aye, that I can understand. I've seen too much of the world, I'm almost tired of it."

His gaze sharpened. "You've told me nothing of yourself, of why you want Devadonides in his grave. I haven't asked, respecting your silence."

For perhaps a dozen paces, Aryalla rode with bowed head. Then she lifted her face, its lovely lines set in grim resolve.

"You should know, Kyrik. Your own history is written in the scrolls of Tantagol, of half our world. All know who care to read, of your victories, of that grim sword you name Bluefang and your repute with its use. Why should you not know of me?

"I was born to a magician named Gorsifal, who practiced his magicks in the city of Antherak. I grew up like any other girl of my times, except that from time to time my father instructed me in the ways of wizards and warlocks, witches and sorceresses. I was fascinated by the lore of demonology, of those nether lands and spaces where dwell such beings as Kilithin and Abakkon. By day and by night I stared at the scrolls, dusty and dry, written in half legible inkings. I scanned the stars, I read the prophetic sticks, the entrails of animals. I did well, before I was twenty.

"Twenty! How long ago that age seems. Yet I am not—too much older, even now." Her black eyes glanced side-wise at the big man almost flirtatiously, and he grinned at her. "Then came a summons from Devadonides, king in Tantagol. He would have my father, who held a certain renown in the necromantic arts from Antherak westward to the sea, labor for him. He offered much gold, so that visions of great wealth danced in my sire's heart and head. We must pack and leave at once, he told me. My mother was dead, we had no other relatives. And love had not touched my heart. What was there to keep me in Antherak?"

"We sold our land, our properties, converting them into griffs. His magical equipment, his alembics and grimoires, his dusty scrolls, his eidolons and thuribles, he packed on our mules. Many and varied were the thaumaturgical utensils of my father, much of them he had inherited from his ancestors who were also great mages."

They were at the city gates now, open before the first incoming wagons and market carts from the outlying farmlands, hurrying to the great square before the housewives and the stewards from the rich houses would arrive to make their selections. Kyrik waved a hand at the guards' captain who grinned back, Aryalla rode with her cloak's hood covering her face, sunk deep in memory.

Between the wagons and the carts, they went at a walk, but when the open road beckoned, dusty and long before them, they touched heels to their mounts' sides and urged them to a canter. The great forests began beyond the farmlands, that lay neat and broad across the vast meadow-lands surrounding the seacoast city. All around them was the rustle and whisper of tall grass and growing crops, the smell of the lush loam and manure, and Kyrik laughed full-throatily as he let the stallion canter.

"Life is sweet, woman," he shouted. He stood in the leather stirrups, nostrils dilating as he drew in every smell, as his eyes touched the roof of a barn, the stone circle of a well. It seemed to Aryalla that he could not experience enough, that he reached out with all his senses for the reassurance that he was alive.

Yet in time, and as the dark forest grew closer, he looked at her. "Tell me more, Aryalla who is a sorceress. You went to Tantagol where Devadonides is king. And there?"

"For a time, my father served Devadonides well. He cast the runes, he searched the stars in the sky, which are said to speak of the future to those who possess the knowledge to understand the astrological wisdoms. Oh, he was well versed in all phases of the black arts. He conjured up demons, commanded them to obey the whims of Devadonides. And the king was well pleased—for a time.

"Oh, the king had other wizards, other warlocks. But none possessed the range of power of my father. He and I would together summon the spirits of the dead to rise from their graves and hold converse with us and with Devadonides."

Well she remembered those nights, with the blustery wind beating rain against the tall tower which Devadonides had given to her father. A howling of the winds, a slashing yellow streaking as lightnings played across the sky—unnatural and alien, as though a part of it were opened to the hell-lands where the demon-gods lived. All this, outside the black stones of the tower; and inside: an evil incantation.

The deep voice of her father, her own clear tones, and the king half crouching in shadows, safe within a pentagram. A gradual smokiness in the air, as of graves pouring out a thick, fetid mist of the charnal regions and in those miasmal fogs, faint figures. Wraith-like they were, swaying as did the mists when a rainy gust would blow between the windows or shrill through a crack in the ancient stones.

Yet they lived, in a fashion. And—they spoke. They told of forgotten treasures, of battles long ago, won or lost. They told Devadonides the secrets of life beyond the grave until he gibbered and wept. And one night they whispered of—Kyrik of the Victories.

"Did they now?" asked the barbarian who had been king of Tantagol.

They were on the forest road, they moved along it at a gallop, their horses' hooves drumming up echoes from the woodland deeps. Wildflowers at the edge of the dusty thoroughfare nodded in the wind of their passing, filling the air with scents that whispered of long, leafy byways and paths in the wild-wood where a man and a maid might linger to kiss and cuddle.

The riders paid these hints no heed, each was immersed in his or her thoughts. It was Kyrik, who stirred, who looked at her and asked, "Why would he wish to speak with Kyrik?"

"His very name is reason enough. Kyrik—of the Victories! No man since his time has so ordered his van, his cavalry, his pikes and bowmen, to achieve the stunning successes he did. A master of the war arts was Kyrik."

"Yet surely his victories are written in the history scrolls?"

"Of course. But they contain so little, nothing of the keen brain that could assess a battle confrontation and make the right moves to snatch stunning victory from apparent defeat. Under Kyrik, the gold and black banners of Tantagol marched where they would—took what they would. As Kyrik had done so would Devadonides do."

"They were empty, all those triumphs," he growled in surly fashion. "They brought a curse on me, a curse that turned me into a six inch high statue for a thousand years."

"Yet now Kyrik is free again. Alive!"

"I am that. But I find no need for kingdoms in me. I want to experience life and what it has to offer, witch-woman! No throne will hold my frame." His huge hand slapped the worn saddle. "This shall be my throne, from now on."

She reached to touch his arm as they galloped, eyes worried. "You will not help me, after I found you and made you live?"

"Oh, aye—I'll help you." Bitterness twisted his lips. "But you don't know the whole tale of my cursing. You see, that other Devadonides made sure I could never unseat him or any of his descendants from the throne that is rightfully mine!"

She stared at him in horror. "What are you saying?" she gasped, after a long moment.

She drew in on her reins, he did the same; they confronted each other beneath the overhanging branches.

His lips twisted in a grim smile. "Your labor's wasted witch-woman I can never do what you ask of me."

"But why? Why?" He shrugged and let his eyes touch the boles of the trees where they framed the roadbed, where they marched in serried ranks deep within the forest, to disappear in a tangle of underbrush and shadows. There was pain in his green eyes, an agony of spirit. Her stare mirrored the despair inside herself as she read the truth of what he said in those eyes.

Her laughter rang out, scornful and mocking. "Two long years I've spent wandering the world to find you in that statue. Time wasted! Time tossed aside as I might throw away a ragged garment."

"Still, we can try," he muttered.

"So that I might die as my father did?"

He let sympathy show on his bronzed face. "Tell me how your

father died, Aryalla—and why. It will serve to pass the time." When he saw her shoulders slump, he reached out, caught her arm and shook it. "Oh, there may be a way—even yet. I said I'd take service with you, and I will."

"I've fought before against odds—almost as great."

As though hope revived her, she nodded faintly. "So be it. Try your best, it's all I can ask. If instead of victory we achieve only defeat, then it was not meant to be."

They rode on, but more slowly, and now Kyrik studied the woodlands on either side of them more carefully, as though he expected danger to confront them in those sunny glades.

Aryalla sighed. "Devadonides asked my father to raise the shade of Kyrik of the Victories, as I've said. No ghost, no phantom, made its appearance. There was only the dark shadows of the tower room, and we three.

"Kyrik is not dead," said my father. "Kyrik lives!" And the king was angry with him, for he believed my father lied, that my father intended to rouse the shade of Kyrik to his own advantage.

"The king went to his other wizards and they raised what they said was the ghost of the former barbarian-king of Tantagol. Aye, they made that phantom talk, caused it to say what Devadonides would hear from its withered lips. And the king sent men to arrest my father."

Before those pike butts pounded on the street level door, however, Gorsifal and Aryalla his daughter had made certain spells and learned from demons who gathered knowledge and wisdom to them as men did riches, that Kyrik had never died, that a conjuration had turned him into a bronze statue and that the statue had been lost from the sight of men for ten times ten centuries of Time. No man, no demon, knew where it was, except that it existed.

The men of King Devadonides had come in the night and taken Gorsifal, dragged him from his warm bed and his sleep, and carried him across the city to the royal gaol. They had tossed him into a cold cell and there they let him lay.

"I was away, that night, visiting a friend," the sorceress whispered. "I heard of what happened and so I hid. King Devadonides did not search for me very long; it was my father who was the wizard, with all the theurgic powers. He did not know that what my sire knew, he had taught me also.

"Disguised, I frequented the taverns, seeking word of my father. I learned," and here her voice broke and she wept a little, "that they had tortured him, long and with sustained cruelty, until he became almost a mindless thing. For weeks the cloak-shrouded executioners of the king worked on his poor body with hot coals and pincers, with flaying knives and metal-barbed whips. They could not break his spirit, they could learn nothing of Kyrik nor of me from his slashed lips.

"And on a day they took him to the high ground called Golgorra in Tantagol City, and there they hung him between four strong horses. The horses pulled off his arms and his legs and the stump of his body fell to the ground and lay there, still quivering with life, until it bled to death."

Aryalla bowed her head, gnawed with strong teeth at her knuckles.

"Devadonides shall pay," Kyrik muttered. "Ah, but how? If you cannot help—you on whom I counted so much—what can anyone do?"

"There is always hope." They went on in silence, but from time to time Aryalla clenched her white hands into fists and sometimes she pounded one on the pommel of her wooden saddle. Kyrik did not look at her, his eyes were on the forest and the road ahead. His sun-bronzed face was set in grim lines, his lips were a thin slash, but his green eyes glowed.

The woman eyed him from time to time, black brows drawn together. To her way of thinking, he seemed to have forgotten her and her tale. He was more interested in the swaying of the branches about them, sniffing the wind that came between the hazel thickets and the tree-boles. It seemed to her brooding eyes that he had no thought save for the wild-wood that encircled them.

Aryalla opened her mouth to protest his indifference.

His upraised hand held her speechless. Kyrik whispered, "Do not show alarm, but we are watched. There are men in these woods. They creep closer, closer..."

They rode on, questions quivering on her mouth. "Are they mere bandits?" the barbarian asked. "Or do they come from Devadonides? He has wizards serving him, you say. Can they have sniffed out the magic that brought me back to life?"

Sunlight winked on an arrowhead. Aryalla shivered.

Chapter 3

A flood of shouting men came out of the woods. Kyrik laughed, a bull bellow of mirth, as his hand lifted out his sword. It made a silver streak in the air as he moved it to knock a hastily nocked arrow to one side. Then he was yanking at his cloak, wrapping it about his left arm, a cloth shield against the bite of arrow-points

"Ride, girl—ride!" he shouted.

She needed no urging, her heels were hammering the mare's ribs, startling it into a gallop. Ahead of her was Kyrik, his broad mailed back hiding her from the men drawing bows at them so that the very air seemed filled with flying shafts.

Bluefang moved in that air, hit the arrows, knocked them to one side. Then, so swiftly did the black stallion run, Kyrik was leaning from the saddle and swinging his blue steeled blade as though it were a feather in his huge hand.

Steel sheared through metal and flesh.

Men went down, by ones, by twos. A path was opening before them on the dusty road. Kyrik was turning, waving his bloody sword at her, yelling at her to gallop. She needed no further urging, she ducked her head close to the whipping mane of the mare and let the frightened beast run.

Aryalla pounded along that road until she reached its crown. Then she sensed she was alone, and reined in, turning her head.

She cried out in surprise. Kyrik had not come with her. He was back there in the road, using that great sword of his as a flail, slicing and slashing at an arm, a hand, a head. The stallion moved as though it understood the needs of its rider, it back-stepped away from a swordsman who came too close, it reared to lash out at a man with iron hooves.

"Fool! Oh, fool!" she cried. Yet even as she named him, Aryalla knew he could no more help staying behind and fighting than she could help her running. Kyrik was a warrior of warriors, or so the legends said. He was a fighting man, in his hands a sword—that long, wicked Bluefang—was as much a part of him as his hand and head.

And as she watched, seeing how he ducked his tawny head to avoid a sword-slash, as he returned that blow with unerring aim and swung aside to cut down another foe, she understood why the history scrolls of Tantagol were filled with his deeds. He had been a fighting king, this man, he had led his banners to victory after victory. He had not hidden in his walled palaces as was the custom of Devadonides, to send other and braver men out upon the field of battle.

Kyrik had gone before his men, not after them.

The woman sensed the love of battle that surged in his veins. She could make out the faint smile on his lips, saw the flash of his green eyes, watched the terrible might of his heavily thewed body as it rained his sword-edge down on those who crowded about him.

So fast did he move, so swift were the reactions of his black stallion to the pressures of knees and toes, that he seemed not one man but two; even, at certain times when he seemed to blur in her eyes, like three. There was a clanging of steel as sword met sword, a swirl of dust and men screaming. . .

Then Kyrik was riding toward her, swiftly, erect in the saddle, cleansing his bloodied blade upon his cloak. His face was alight with pleasure, his grin was broad.

"By the dead gods of Ilfeakol—I needed that," he laughed.

"You might have been killed," she scolded. "What? By a handful of bowmen? Girl, learn one thing about Kyrik now: he is a child of battle. I was born on a bloody field, I could ride when I was two, swing a real sword when I was six."

"Besides, bowmen on foot are poor foes to a mounted warrior. They're not swordsmen for the most part, and if you crowd them, not giving them time to let off their shafts, they're almost helpless. I made them use their swords, you see. By using their swords against me, they were giving me the advantage."

She eyed him with a vague wonder. "They outnumbered you! I don't know by how many, but they did."

"And I was on a horse. By the gods, a good horse, too. I'll keep this one. I've a feeling he was trained to hold a fighting man. Now, ride, girl. I've slain a number of them, wounded others—but there are those who still live, who'll come running after us when they regroup their little force. I don't want an arrow in my spine."

He led the way, making the black gallop with the mare coming at its rump. He stood in the leather stirrups, glancing behind him, laughing. He was a big, vital man; Aryalla sensed he was relishing this brush with death, the danger he faced. There were men like that, she knew, who only enjoyed life when it was threatened by black death.

They rode along the dusty highway for many miles. Yet still the forest was around them, growing darker as the sun set to the west, blackening the shadows of the trees and adding to the gloom of the wood. Now the iron hooves of their horses struck sparks from rocks as the road became more stony. Kyrik reined in, glanced at the ground.

"Here we can move off the road into the wild-wood! Those who follow us can't see our tracks because this pebbled stuff won't take hoof-marks!"

He turned the stallion, was gone between two trees. Aryalla cried out, urged the mare after him. Twenty feet inside the forest, the barbarian sat his saddle, grinning.

"I know these woods, in my time they were known as the Hanging Trees because a predecessor of mine hung a number of rebels on their branches. There's a small cottage not too far away—if it still exists."

He went along a path between tree-boles, beneath low-hanging branches that brushed his head and shoulders. The woman followed silently, letting the mare pick her own trail. She took time to note how the caroling of birds about them and the faint rustle of the leaves in an errant breeze were peaceful sounds. It was hard to believe, deep in these woods, that men had tried to kill her short moments before.

Her gaze touched Kyrik, studying his broad back, his easy sway to the movements of his mount. He rode with his left hand on his sword-hilt; to silence the rattle of the scabbard-chains, she realized. Aye, he was a woodsman, too. Deeper into these copses and glades he went, and swiftly, considering how thick the trees were growing, how tangled the underbrush.

The sun was setting, a reddish haze was on the land. Soon it would be twilight. Already she could see the two moons above, and a star glittering here and there in the pale blue sky. Aryalla shivered. It would be a cold, uncomfortable night in this wild-wood!

Water gurgled. They came to a spring, moved across it. Kyrik, turned in the saddle, resting a hand on the cantle. "It isn't far now, the cottage, just a little more."

Out of her tiredness and tautened nerves she snapped, "That cottage you speak of existed a thousand years ago. Today it is nothing but rotted wood—if, indeed, that wood hasn't become compost on the forest floor."

"Na, na, girl. That cottage was my hunting lodge, built of—ha! Look for yourself." His mailed arm pointed and she gasped.

The lodge was built of field-stones, low to the ground and with a door and two windows visible on this side. Its roof had been thatched, long ago. It was rotted, but still serviceable enough, she supposed, overhung with tree-branches that would shelter it from rain in the summer and from the snows of winter. Bushes hid much of the lower structure and a dirt path overgrown by weeds was visible before the doorway, where a stone slab was laid. A thick stone chimney rose upward from the roof.

Kyrik swung from the saddle, turned to assist the sorceress. "We'll sleep here the night, be on our way with the dawn," he told her.

She slipped from her horse, came down into his outstretched arms. He felt her warm and soft, enjoyed the feel of her body against his own. For an instant his arms tightened about her, holding her close.

When her black eyes stared up at him questioningly, he grinned, "A thousand years is a long time without a woman, Aryalla. I find a sudden love for life and the delights that life can bring to a man, inside myself."

"We have more important things to do," she said curtly, freeing herself.

He watched her go, shaking his head. His head lifted, he stared up at the darkling sky, the tree-branches. Aye, he had been a long time dead-alive. His lungs drew in the scents of the woodlands, he heard the rustle of a wild animal between the stalks of the berry-bushes. These were the simple pleasures, the sight of sky and tree, the scent of clean air, the sense of stirring life all about him. Kyrik found a new enjoyment in them.

He went after the woman, pushed open the door, stepped with her into cool dimness. His stare ranged the big room, touching the fireplace, the heavy wooden table and the chairs set before it, the worn rug on the floor. There were cheeses and fruits hanging in nets from an overhead beam, there was a log placed with dried twigs below it in the fireplace that took up almost all of one wall.

The barbarian loosed the dagger in his scabbard. "Someone's been living here," he growled, and went to prowl about the room.

On either side of the cabin were beds sunk into the frame of the walls, low and broad. In those other years, he had slept here, sometimes with a hunting companion, more often alone. He knew this room as he knew the back of his hand. Now one bed had a blanket on it, the other a mattress. Kyrik scowled.

There was no dust on the table or the chairs, someone had used a twig broom to sweep the floor. Kyrik moved toward one of the hanging trees, tore it down, tossed it to the woman.

"At least we'll eat when we get hungry."

"Suppose the—the occupant of this place comes back?"

"He'll have to fight me for it. It belongs to me."

"A thousand years ago. A thousand years is a long time, Kyrik."

He stared at her. "Are you saying I have no rights to the place? As I have no right to the throne Devadonides now holds? I say I do I say the lodge is mine, the throne is mine—if I want it."

"If you want it?" His broad shoulders lifted, fell. "A throne can be an anchor to a man. Oh, I'll not desert you in your quest for vengeance. I owe Devadonides something for what his ancestor did to me. But otherwise. . ."

He shrugged again, went to touch spark to tinder to light a flame under the log. His eyes watched the tiny flame grow into a fire, saw that fire begin to eat at the log. Outside the cottage the night was closing a blackness about the woodlands, and a cold wind was springing up.

They ate the cheese, speaking only rarely. When they were done, his hand gestured at the blanketed bed. "You sleep there. The mattress is good enough for me. I've slept in worse places."

Her black eyes bored into his. "My head tells me you'll not sleep too well, this night. You expect a visitor, don't you?"

He rasped laughter. "The thought occurred to me. I'll be ready for him."

Thunder rumbled in the distance. Through the narrow-paned windows they could see flashes of lightning across a blackened sky. In a little while the first raindrops fell, spattering on the thatched roof, hissing against the windows. The room was warm, comfortable. The flames were licking all about the log, the twigs burned away.

Aryalla rose, drew her cloak more tightly around her. Her head nodded at the blanketed bed. Kyrik sat unmoving, hunched over the cheese in its netting, his long dagger close to his hand. His eyes touched her hips as she moved away, then slid sideways toward the door.

He waited with the patience of an animal as the woman made herself comfortable with the blanket thrown over her. The storm was worsening, the rain was coming down in sheets, blowing against the little windows as gusts of air drove it in wet squalls. Inside the cottage, the fire crackled and a knot in the log popped. And still Kyrik did not move.

Yet his ears were ready for the cry when it came from the depths of the forest, he heard and assessed it, stirred and put his hand on the pommel of the dagger. He rose soundlessly, moved toward the door, opened it a little. The rain came in, but he paid no attention to it. All his senses were alerted to the black wetness beyond the cottage.

Aryalla asked, "What is it? I'm awake, I heard the cry."

He did not turn his head. "Who knows? It sounded like—but that cannot be." His head turned, the firelight touched his green eyes, making them red. "Go to sleep."

"Who can sleep? And don't order me around." He chuckled. "Was I ordering? I didn't know."

"You always order. Don't you know that? It's a habit of yours. You do always what you want to do. You never ask me what I might think."

He turned back to the door. The sounds were louder, someone was blundering in panic-stricken haste between the tree-boles It seemed to the man standing motionless by the door that he heard something whimper, out there. His hand tightened on the dagger-hilt

Something flung itself against the door. Someone—cried out.

Kyrik threw open the door, reached forth, caught a slim wrist and yanked. A girl came flying into the room, stumbling and wailing as she fought to recover her balance. Her leg hit a chair, she skidded and fell.

The barbarian slammed the door shut, dropped the latch into place and put his shoulders to the wood.

The girl was half lying, half crouched on the worn rug. There was a poniard in her brown hand. Tumbled brown hair was plastered to an oval face in which brown eyes glared up at him and full red lips hung open. She wore a torn skirt with a laced leather bodice over a blouse that clung to her wet skin. The skirt had been ripped away so that it did little more than cover her upper thighs.

"Who are you?" she whispered. "The owner of this hunting lodge." She gawked at him, then uttered harsh laughter. "Nobody owns this place! It's why I use it—to hide when my services aren't needed by the Romanoys."

"And who are these Romanoys?" She eyed him more closely. "Where've you been, you've never heard of the Romanoy gypsies? We're wanderers, we range the woodlands and the high hills, we keep to ourselves for the most part."

Slowly, as though not to alarm him, she put a hand to the nearby table, yanked herself to her feet. Her clothes were sopping, they clung to her lissome body, revealing all its shapeliness. Kyrik let his eyes run over her, studied the exposed breasts where the bodice lacings had come undone. "Who's after you?" he asked. "A guards officer. One of Devadonides' men who saw me at the Fair this day and followed me."

Kyrik smiled grimly, "One of Devadonides' mercenaries."

Under sullen brows, she glowered at him. "Aren't you afraid? You know what happens to any who dare lift cold steel against his henchmen."

"I don't know, but it doesn't frighten me." Aryalla snapped, "Don't be a fool, Kyrik We can get away, you and the girl and I. No need to stay here to spill more blood."

The girl whirled, dagger up. Her eyes touched the sorceress where she sat on the edge of the bed, wrapped in her cloak.

"More blood?" she snapped. Her eyes brushed Kyrik.

"A little unpleasantness on the highway this afternoon."

Aryalla added, "He slew a dozen of them." The girl's eyes popped. "By Absothoth. How many men sided you?"

"He did it with that great sword of his—alone. So what need has Kyrik to fear the coming of a lone guards officer?" asked Aryalla almost bitterly.

The girl lowered her dagger hand, brooded at the giant. "There aren't many men left in Tantagol who would dare such a thing, let alone do it. Where are you from?"

Kyrik shrugged. He was studying the shapely brown legs of the girl, her bared shoulders and partially bared breasts, and found her good to look upon. He grinned suddenly, glancing at the sorceress.

"From Tantagol. I've been wandering myself." His suddenly upraised hand held them speechless, frozen. They could hear blundering footsteps, whipping branches. Then a harsh voice hailed the lodge.

"I see the firelight in your cottage, Myrnis! You won't escape me any more."

He came blundering out of the rain, head down. Kyrik opened the door, watched him come nearer. Within a few feet of the yellow rectangle that was the doorway, the officer halted, looked up as though warned by instinct. His mouth fell open.

Kyrik shot out a hand, caught him by his cloak, yanked him stumbling forward. He stepped aside, and as the man began his fall, the barbarian backhanded him across the face. The man fell heavily, lay there.

The girl screeched triumphantly, lifted her dagger and dropped on him. Only Kyrik's hand stopped that cold-blooded slaying, wrapping fingers about her wrist and lifting her up as though she were no more than a rag doll.

"Let me go," she panted, eyes glaring. "I'll slit his weasand for him. By Absothoth. He'll spread the alarm if we let him live!"

Kyrik shook her. "Listen to me, wench I say the man lives—at least, until he can fight for his life. I'll have no hand in murder."

He thrust her back so that her rump hit the table, where she sagged and stared at him. She half raised the dagger but when her eyes met his, she dropped her arm.

"You're a fool! A fool, you understand? That one is more mean, more vicious than any of the others. He's Kangor, captain of the mercenaries. An Ocarian!"

She spat to indicate her fury.

Kyrik waited. Soon the man began to stir, raised his head. He turned, seeing the big barbarian. His eyes went over him slowly, taking in the mail shirt, the long sword at his side, the leather belt and fur kilt. Cautiously, he backed up and rose to his feet.

"I could have you flayed alive for striking a guards officer," he rasped. His hand went to his face, where blood was trickling from his nose.

"In the old days, a guards officer conducted himself like a man, not a beast. Does Devadonides permit his soldiers to rape helpless girls without punishment?"

The officer laughed. "Devadonides is too busy with his spells and incantations to care what his men do. Who are you who doesn't know his ways?"

"A stranger, a wanderer. What does Devadonides seek from his wizards?"

"Who knows? It's rumored he wants to rule the world."

Kyrik grinned. "By using demons?" Kangor stared at him, shrugged. He said, "I'll be going now, since you want the land-loper for yourself." His head jerked at the girl.

"I need sleep, captain. And if I were to turn you loose outside, you'd bring your fellows here to interrupt my dreams. So lie down, like a good fellow, and let me tie you up."

Kangor grinned widely, showing yellow teeth. "By the gods, you're a cool one. Lie down, you say. To me! Now you listen I—"

He leaped, fist out and cudgeling a path toward Kyrik's face. The big man did not seem to move, but he was not there when Kangor leaped, he was sliding sideways and bringing up a fist to the other man's jaw. Kangor's head snapped back, he gave a muffled cry through back-drawn lips. Then he fell like a poled ox.

"Slay him," pleaded the girl. Kyrik knelt, tied the man with his own belt and a few strips from his cloak, that he tore between his big hands. When he was done, the man lay stretched out, bound and gagged.

The barbarian looked up at the gypsy. "I ought to tie you up, as well. Otherwise when I'm asleep, you'll slit his throat."

She shook her head. "No. You helped me this night, I'm not ungrateful. Let him live, if that's the way you want it. I can always kill him when he tries to rape me again." Her dagger gleamed in the firelight as she moved it viciously.

Kyrik lay down on the floor, put his hand behind his head. "Go to sleep in the free bed, girl. The floor is good enough for me."

She stood over him and frowned. She sighed, clicked her dagger into the scabbard at her side, hanging from a belt. "My name is Myrnis."

Hips swaying, she walked away. Kyrik eyed her a moment, closed his eyes. A blazing knot popped in the fireplace. The rain came down, harder even than before, and lightning streaked across the black sky where thunder rolled a moment later. Slowly, the fire died out. . .

Morning sunlight showed Kyrik the beamed ceiling when he opened his eyes. Instantly he put hand to his dagger hilt, rolled over to stare around him. The trussed guards officer lay sleeping; during the night he had rolled toward the fire, apparently in an attempt to burn his bonds on the red coals. Kyrik had the suspicion that the rain coming down the chimney had put out those coals before he could do what he planned.

The room was cold without the fire. Kyrik rose to stir up the ashes, start a new one. Then he saw that the mattress was empty. The gypsy girl had gone.

He roused Aryalla with a gentle hand. Her eyes snapped open, she sat up. "The girl's run off. It's time for us to ride. We'll leave him lying here. If someone finds him, he'll live. If not. . ."

The barbarian turned away. Aryalla rose from the bed, wrapped her cloak about her and moved toward the table. She lifted the cheese, tucked it under her cloak. Then she walked after Kyrik into the sun dappled woods.

He was standing motionless, hand on his sword. "What now?" she asked. "Men come. By Illis! This isn't a friendly world I've come back to. Everyone is always attacking, it seems."

"We could mount and ride," she suggested. He shook his head

almost imperceptibly. "Too late. They're near, they'd see us. I'd rather fight than run, anyhow."

The gypsy girl came first, carrying two rabbits. She had donned a new blouse that hid her breasts, but her skirt was still the torn one she had worn last night. She had combed her brown hair, it hung down on either side of her piquant face.

Four men followed her, wearing woolen tunics with animal-skin capes on their shoulders; big gold rings swung from their ears. Wool leggins were strapped tightly to avoid tearing in the thick underbrush. Each gypsy carried a short bow, a dagger at his belt, a quiver of arrows over a shoulder.

They halted at sight of him. The girl came on, smiling.

"I brought you breakfast. I also brought help, in case it might be needed."

"My thanks, Myrnis." Her smile widened. "What of Kangor?" When he told her, she nodded. "Yes, leave him to the gods. Or demons. If one or the other want him, they can have him. Come, get your horses and follow me. We go deeper into the woods."

Aryalla walked a little behind the gypsy girl, with Kyrik following, leading their horses. The four men trailed after the barbarian, their eyes moving between the trees, scanning the darkest shadows. The morning sunlight filtered between the leafy branches; there was a coolness and a silence in these woods that only their own sounds disturbed as they paced along a game trail.

When they came to a little copse where green grass grew between bordering trees, Myrnis held up a hand. Kyrik moved to stand beside her.

"I've been thinking," she told him, frowning. "You can't go marching into Tantagol City in those garments. You have the look of a warrior, it's written all over you. And they clap strange warriors in the dungeons, in Tantagol town."

Kyrik grinned, "I've been thinking much the same thing, myself."

Her brown eyes went over him boldly. "You might be made into a gypsy, a Romanoy, with walnut juice to stain your skin and big gold rings in your ears."

"And what good would such masquerade do me?"

"There's a fair on. The people welcome the wanderers. We do tricks for them, to make them laugh." Her brown eyes mocked him. "Can you do tricks, Kyrik?"

His laughter rang out. "Aye, girl. I know a stunt or two will open their eyes. By Illis, I do!"

"Come then, walk with me and plan our garb. And speak to me of this stunt you can do so well."

Aryalla was frowning at the Romanoy girl, the barbarian saw, and chuckled to himself. It would serve the sorceress right if she thought Myrnis was making a play to get him into her cot of nights. He walked close to Myrnis as they moved through the woods, and from time to time his arm went about her slim middle, holding her soft body warm against his as he swung her over a rock or across a rippling brook. And Myrnis laughed and flirted with him, every step of the way.

Chapter 4

They saw the wagon first, a weather-beaten contraption with warped wooden sides and roof, but painted bright colors, set upon four big wheels. It rested in a forest glade, with others like it not too far away. These Romanoys were new to Kyrik, in his time there had been no wanderers such as this, and he wanted to know more about them.

"In time, in time," Myrnis promised as she walked with him toward that wagon. "First you must be made into a gypsy fellow, a vagrant with a brightly colored band about that tawny hair of yours. Mmmmm, we'll have to dye it black, too. But when I'm done, even your woman won't know you."

Her head jerked at Aryalla. Kyrik chuckled, "No woman of mine. We're partners, is all. Now, let's to business."

"Inside my wagon, then."

He went up the few wooden steps, bent to move into cool dimness. Myrnis swung in after him, turned to lift a wooden chest inside which were stop leather bottles of varying liquids. Her eyes stared at him gleefully.

"Strip down, giant," she laughed. And when he was naked, his mail shirt and fur kilt forgotten on the floor, the girl nodded in delight. "A real man, by all the old gods. When I'm done with you, you'll be a man I'd be proud to call my chal."

"Chal? What's that mean?"

"Lover," she smiled slyly, and pouring dark juice on her cupped palm, began to smear it over his flesh.

She stood close to him, perfumed and warm, bare flesh under the thin blouse and torn skirt, with the laced bodice that did little more than push her breasts up into the blouse. Kyrik could not help his male reaction to her nearness and she laughed softly, knowing it.

"You've been a long time without a woman, warrior," she giggled.

A thousand years, he thought. He said, "You speak the truth, girl. A long time."

"Well, the gypsies are hot-blooded, you'll fit right in."

When she was done, he saw in a cracked mirror she lugged into view that he was like a bronzed statue once again. His flesh was a pale brown, his green eyes stood out with startling clarity in his face. And when she smeared black juices into his hair and mustache, and affixed gold earrings to his ears, no man could have said he was not a true Romanoy.

He dressed in loose shirt and breeks, with a rope belt. Over his head he wore a red bandanna, set at an angle. Aryalla did not know him when he stepped from the wagon. Her eyes went this way and that about the camp until he sank beside her and said, "There, now. I have a way of entering Tantagol City. What about you?"

Her eyes grew big as they searched his face. She nodded. "Yes. No one would ever guess you for Kyrik. It will be a good disguise. I shall do the same."

Myrnis would not smear on the juices for her as she had done for Kyrik. She handed over the wooden coffer and let her go into the wagon by herself. When she was gone, Myrnis caught Kyrik by a hand and drew him with her toward the woods.

"There is a woodland shrine deep in these trees," she murmured. "Often I come there to whisper prayers to Illis."

Kyrik showed surprise. "To Illis? Yet Illis is not a goddess of the forests."

"Still, there is an altar of sorts built to her. Come, see for yourself."

And when they had moved between the tree-boles, stepped across two little streams and had come to a small glade where the sunlight gleamed like gold, Kyrik saw the shrine. It was of stones laced together with mortar in the shape of a seashell, and on the flat stone that served as an altar he saw a rectangle of what seemed to be glass. It was colorless, dead, yet he knew that at one time it might have gleamed with life.

"Illis is dead," he said hoarsely. She eyed him thoughtfully. "Now how can you know that, warrior? It's true that that glass, that bit of substance, is allied to the goddess of the flesh lusts. I've heard legends about the thing from the charcoal burners who live in the high hills behind here and come to worship, from time to time. How did you know?"

"I too worship Illis." His hand fumbled in the belt purse which he had transferred from his sword-belt to the length of rope about his middle now. "Turn away, Myrnis. This jewel I'm uncovering has—strange powers."

His hand took it out, placed it on the glass rectangle. Myrnis stared at it, entranced. The red gem seemed to be on fire deep inside. She stared at a naked woman, a tiny simulacra of a living woman, who twisted and turned in lascivious poses. Waves of that desire beat out of her, touched her womanhood, her body.

Her hand caught his arm. "Kyrik. . ."

"Turn away your eyes!"

"I cannot Kooshti duuvell! What is that thing?"

"It is the Lust-stone, it belongs to Illis." Now the glass rectangle came to life. It grew lighter, it glowed with pearly luminescence. And a faint, sensuous music came from its depths. Music that throbbed in the air, that stirred the blood in both man and woman. The rectangle coruscated, it whispered with arpeggios of sweetness. It flooded the air, the forest glade where they stood. Myrnis shivered.

A sweet voice whispered, "Who is this who holds the Lust-stone?"

"I do, Illis of the tinted breasts."

"That voice I know it. From long and long ago, when it was raised in worship of my beauty. Yes, yes. This is Kyrik. Kyrik of the Victories. You have been-long dead, Kyrik."

"Under a spell, great Illis." There was a silence. Then: "Yes. Cast by Devadonides, aided by his wizard Jokaline. I could not prevent it, I was powerless in your world without the Lust-stone! Yet now. . ."

Triumph throbbed in that godlike throat. "Yet now, Kyrik Place you the Lust-stone where it was meant to be, and I shall be your protector once again. How did you find it?"

"Long ago, I knew a thief. The thief I caught, and caused to be tortured until he told me where he hid the jewel—I set out to get it, to place it on your altar and—was turned into a six inch high bronze statue. A sorceress named Aryalla searched for me, found me and restored me to life."

"Blessed be Aryalla. I shall not forget." Kyrik caught Myrnis where she huddled against him, shivering. She was moving her palms over his chest, sliding her hands into the blouse so she might caress his massive chest. With a hand about her arm, he swung her toward the rectangle that was glowing a deep rose.

"This one helped too, Illis. Keep her well."

"I see. I shall throw my mantle about her." Myrnis stared with wide eyes at the glass embedded in the stone altar. Before it was the Lust-stone, red and brilliant, flaring to that power which was inside it. She moved back against the barbarian, used his body as a leaning post, so weak had her knees become. Then the rose color faded, the glass emptied of its power. Kyrik, aware of the girl who pressed her softness against him, reached for the Lust-stone, wrapped the kerchief about it, thrust it into his purse.

"Who are you?" she whimpered, turning and throwing her arms about his neck. "Who is Kyrik of the Victories? You said the stone was stolen—a long time ago. How long? And what you said about being a statue? Can that be true?"

His mouth covered her soft lips.

She arched against him, felt his hands slide down her back to grip at her buttocks, to lift and hold her against him. She felt the power and the might of him and this touch did what the Lust-stone had begun.

"Take me, Kyrik. Take me!"

"In worship of Illis?"

"Yes, yes, yes. . ."

He drew her down with him upon the grass.

Later, when the shadows were lengthening, Myrnis drew the blouse about her nakedness, for the sun was setting and the day had grown chill. There was a glistening in her eyes where tears of happiness gathered, and she bent her head to kiss his lips, gently.

"I've never known a chal like you," she breathed. "A thousand years is a long time, girl. I find myself new-born into a world that has changed while I was gone. There is a need to enjoy life inside me, not from the throne where I once sat but out here in this wild-wood or in a town tavern, where red wine warms a man's insides."

His hand tousled her brown hair that hung long about her shoulders and veiled her breasts. "This is life, this sharing of our bodies, this rapture of the senses. I find a need for it in me."

"So soon—again?" she asked slyly. He rumbled laughter. "Na, na. Not now. But again, yes." He stared up at the darkening sky. "For now, I must go into Tantagol, and place the Lust-stone in its place, if I'm ever to succeed against Devadonides." He sighed, "I had not thought it possible, I believed Illis to have gone back into her own worlds after so long a time—and without her help, I could never do what must be done. So the Lust-stone goes to Illis."

"Couldn't you keep it, just a little longer?"

"I need it not. Do you?" Myrnis laid her head on his bared chest, whispering, "Not I. It's enough just to have you near me."

"Come, then. I'm starving." She rose and pulled her skirt about her, watched as he slid into the Romanoy garments he had discarded. Then her small hand sought his larger one and clasped it all the way back to the gypsy camp between the trees.

The moon was in the sky and the smell of roasting pig was in the air as they came to the fire where Aryalla crouched, staring into the flames. She did not raise her eyes, she merely nodded when they halted near her.

"You used the Lust-stone—with her," she whispered.

"I only fight for you, woman." Her eyelids lifted and Kyrik was surprised at the heat and fury in them. By Illis. If she came to his bed with that fire showing, she might prove to be an even better bed-mate than the gypsy girl. She turned her head and sorceress and Romanoy girl stared hard at one another. Jealousy flared between them so Kyrik clapped a hand to the gypsy's behind, half lifting her off her feet.

"I starve, Myrnis," he growled. She laughed and ran to slice pork for him, and a heap of steaming beans flavored with spices. She ran back and seated herself beside him, handing him the plate.

"Eat, then—lover." Aryalla hissed. Yet they ate together that night in seeming friendship, though the sorceress said little. Myrnis could not have enough of waiting upon Kyrik, bringing him a wine-skin chilled in a cold brook. She watched as he drank deep, arms clasped about her knees.

"I shall dance for you," she told him. "Na, na. Tomorrow will be a hard day, girl. Save your strength—as I intend to hoard my own."

He rose to his feet, caught up a horse blanket, and walked toward the edge of the forest. He stretched out like a big animal, and was soon asleep.

Myrnis stood, looked down at the sorceress. With a sniff, she walked to where the man lay and curled up beside him. Aryalla watched them for a long time, then with a faint smile, came up from the ground to join them. She lay down on the other side of the man, and tossed an arm about him.

Kyrik woke to the touch of two female bodies, with a shaft of sunlight tickling his eyelids. He lay a moment, remembering, then lifted on an elbow, turning to stare at the gypsy girl where she lay doubled up, smiling faintly in her sleep. He swung about to look at Aryalla, her curving red mouth and long-lashed eyelids.

He grunted and slid from between them, moved to the campfire, put new branches on the coals, watched them flare to flame. By this time, the camp was stirring; Myrnis and Aryalla had come to lend their hands with the cooking.

"We leave soon," Myrnis said, gnawing on a bone. "We're due in Tantagol within the hour." She viewed Kyrik tenderly. "Are you sure you can perform tricks that will draw a crowd and put silver rhodanthes in our wallets?"

Kyrik nodded, too busy eating to answer. Aryalla laughed softly. "Watch me, gypsy." There were horses for them to ride, and as they swung up, Myrnis said again to Aryalla, "That black cloak you wear. It's morbid. People like to see gypsies in gay colors. There's enough drabness in their lives because of Devadonides."

The sorceress put a hand to the silver clasp that held her cloak. It slid away from her. Kyrik drew a deep breath, staring. She wore gypsy garments, a torn blouse that showed her full breasts, a tattered skirt that bared the loveliness of her legs. His eyes slid toward Myrnis who was biting her lip and scowling. Kyrik laughed, head thrown back, hanging the sack with his mail shirt and weapons about the saddle pommel by a thong.

"She shows a real woman, Myrnis," he grinned. "Ride," the gypsy cried, and banged heels to her mount.

They cantered along the dusty road that wound between the trees of the Hanging Forest. Here and there, where the woodlands had been cleared, they could see neat farmhouses and fields of waving grain, of corn, of growing things. Carts were creaking, too, laden with vegetables and fruit for the city marketplaces.

Where the road made a bend and straightened for the city gates, Kyrik saw the city itself, broad and wide, with high stone walls and leaded roof tiles glittering in the early morning sun. This was a bigger, larger city than he remembered from those days when he had ruled here in the palace whose spires rose upward toward the sky.

They rode more slowly, for the dusty road was crowding now with farm wagons and with carts, there were people walking along the sides of the road, and here and there were mountebanks and strolling players cavorting and strumming tunes upon their harps. Kyrik let his eyes rove to the tinkling bells of a jester in red and yellow, he peeped down the low-cut bodice of a passing girl, spying out her pale breasts, he tossed a coin to a carter for a leathern jack filled with foaming ale.

He sniffed in the smells of human sweat and dusty road, the fragrance of the wildflowers bordering the highway. This was life. This was why a man was born, to drink at the wine of living, at the pleasures —aye, and even at the pains it brought. Otherwise, a man was a dead thing. As he had been dead, for a thousand years.

In this flush of enthusiasm, he touched the crenelated walls and towers of the grim barbarian and adjoining keep of Tantagol with his eyes, recognizing them from the days when he had ruled this world about him. Newer walls had been added over the centuries, the old city was ringed in by a newer. Sunlight winked on the helmets and spearpoints of the soldiers who strode the wall walkways, who were clustered outside the open city gates. None challenged, none suspected, as he rode over cobblestones into the city. He followed Myrnis, letting her lead the way, swaying gracefully in the saddle she straddled. Aryalla stayed close to his left, her bared leg brushing his upon occasion, when the press about them grew too thick.

Along a main thoroughfare the gypsy took them to a great city square in which colored booths had been set up, where fruits and vegetables were displayed on long boards, in wicker baskets. Here Myrnis swung from her saddle but Kyrik sat a moment, head turned so that he might see the great castle that towered above the city on what had been a hill covered with flowers in ancient times. His heart thudded in his rib-cage. He knew those walls. Often at night he had stared from those arrow-slits, looking out over the city and the land that owed him allegiance. Another sat his throne, another had taken it from him by sorcery. By Illis! His descendant should not keep it long.

Myrnis said, "Now live up to your boasts, Kyrik. Amuse us!"

The crowds recognized the gypsy girl, the other Romanoys with her. They called for her to dance, for the men to turn cartwheels.

Myrnis cried out, laying a hand on Kyrik's foot where the stirrup held it, "Another comes to amuse you this day, a woodlands stranger. And with him, a woman who has sworn to delight you."

Kyrik looked around him, saw an archer leaning on a longbow. "You, friend. A loan of your bow, your arrows."

The man laughed, tossed them. Kyrik came down off his horse, caught Myrnis and swung her so that her back was to a wooden table that was set on end before being righted to hold offerings for sale. The tabletop rested on its narrow end, its height was greater than that of the gypsy girl.

"Move not," he told her. He ran fifty paces away, whirled and set arrow to bow. An instant later that arrow thudded into the tabletop, just grazing her hip. Her brown eyes glared at him, but she stood proudly, unwilling to show fear. Again and again he shot, so swiftly that the eyes could not follow his movements. And when he was done, Myrnis was ringed about with arrows sunk deep into the wood.

The awed archer stared at him, making the sign of Abakkon in the air. "What manner of man are you, who can shoot so true and so swiftly? I've never seen anybody draw bow like that."

Kyrik pulled the arrows from the tabletop, tossed them toward the bowman who slid them into his quiver. "A master of weapons, at sword and dagger, at bow and pike, I take no back step to any man."

"Devadonides would give much to see you in his guard."

Kyrik shrugged. "I like the free life, the wandering from city to city. No walls shall hem me in."

Myrnis was scampering about, picking up coins that had been thrown in appreciation of the show Kyrik had put on. Aryalla in her torn gypsy dress was at her side, helping.

"What does the black-haired one do?" asked the archer, unstringing his bow.

"Aryalla," Kyrik called. "Show the man!"

The sorceress walked toward the bowman, put a hand to his ear, drew out a wriggling, twisting snake. Men and women cried out on seeing this, they stared and drew closer. Aryalla laughed, tossed the snake high—the onlookers saw it change into a stick of solid gold—and caught it with a deft hand as it came down.

Myrnis pressed to Kyrik. "How did she do that?"

"A trick of conjuring. Nothing more." Aryalla was breaking the gold stick, snapping it, turning each broken portion into a bit of sweetmeat that she tossed to the gawking onlookers. The more she broke off, however, the longer the gold stick was becoming. It grew even as she snapped it.

Myrnis was muttering, "She's a witch!"

Kyrik pinched her rump. "Enough of that talk!" Coins were falling at Aryalla's bare feet. Kyrik pushed Myrnis, said, "Go pick up the money. Get rich."

Common sense took hold of the Romanoy girl. She nodded, ran. And while the sorceress made more sweetmeats and then still more, Myrnis busied herself in gathering up the money flung in testimony of the crowd's enjoyment.

Eventually Aryalla tired, threw the golden stick high. It glittered, turned into a puff of smoke, blew away. Kyrik caught her hand, drew her out of the crowd toward his black stallion. He took down the sack in which were his mail shirt and weapons.

"Let the gypsies perform now," he told her. "We have work to do."

"What work?"

"I must get inside the palace."

"Join the guard. That bowman as good as invited you.

His teeth glistened as he grinned. "A slow process. I've a better. I'll get myself arrested."

The sorceress whirled on him. "Are you mad? Do you know what they do to prisoners in Tantagol City? They are beheaded."

"What? For a harmless little drunkenness? Na, na. Even this Devadonides cannot be so stupid."

She glared at him, white hands clenched into fists. "You fool! You promised to help me. Is this the way of your helping? To get yourself tossed into a dungeon?"

"I've given it thought," he told her, urging her to turn and walk with him by a hand on her elbow. "I can scarcely go before the king and proclaim him to be an impostor and myself the rightful ruler."

"But—the dungeons!"

"I know then—inside and out. Aye! There's no part of the old stone walls that have not known my foot, in times long forgotten. Now come along, like a good girl. You'll be my excuse for a quarrel."

"Not I!" she exclaimed, and pulled free. When she would have fled, he cried out, "Wait! What will you be doing while I'm in gaol? How can I find you when I need you?"

"I have a hiding place. I'll whisper it to Myrnis. When you need me, come to me. I'll be waiting."

She turned and ran as if he were a madman. And may-hap I am, thought Kyrik, smiling wryly, staring after her. And yet, this is the one thing that must be done, if ever I can hope to pull Devadonides off his golden throne. Aryalla does not know it, nor Myrnis, nor any living man or woman; but the way to topple Devadonides lies within the stone walls of his cellar ways.

He laughed and examined the few coins in his belt purse. Enough for a wine-skin and a leathern jack or two or ale. Enough to pretend to be drunk, most certainly. He walked on, found that the twisting streets of this older city were shaping themselves in his mind once more, as they had been long ago.

At a corner where a wooden sign in the shape of an ale barrel hung on creaking chains, he turned aside, entered the cool dimness. He staggered in his gait, he saw sharp-eyed men stiffen, saw the blowsy women near the bar break into smiles at sight of this drunken gypsy. A chicken running to its plucking, a drunk about to be robbed. He was no more than that in their eyes. He paid silver rhodanthes for a bulging wine-skin, carried it to a dark corner where he began drinking steadily. The men and women watched him, their eyes unblinking. Once a woman crossed the sawdust floor to him, offered to bed him down in an upstairs room. Kyrik pushed her away, muttered thickly that he wanted no woman, all he wanted was the wine-skin! He dozed, after a time, the skin half full.

It was now that the sharp-eyed men glanced at one another, rose to their feet. They came at him slowly, from all directions, sauntering leisurely. Not until they were three feet away did they leap.

Hands closed on his arms, to hold him. Other hands reached for his belt purse. And Kyrik rose up, bellowing happily, and his fingers clamped like iron vises on wrists and forearms. Some men he slung over the table, others he caught with his left hand and hammered at their faces with his right fist. A man broke a chair over his broad back. Kyrik caught that man by his hair and pounded his head against the tabletop. He grabbed a foot that would have kicked him and twisted it, snapping an ankle. Ten men had come at him, five lay moaning on the floor, the other five were trying to turn and flee.

And Kyrik would not permit them. He was savoring the joys of battle, there was a grim smile on his mouth even as his knuckles bloodied faces and his massive hands snapped bones. He drove now—terrified men into tables and chairs, splintering wood.

"By Illis!" he roared. "Fight, man, fight!" And again: "Call yourselves thieves and robbers, do you? In my time such as you would be no more than beggars. Aye, Tantagol City has fallen on lean and awful days under Devadonides!"

He toyed with them, not hurrying, enjoying the battle that raged the length and breadth of the tavern. And when the doorway was darkened by the city watchmen drawn to the ale house by the sound of shattering furniture, Kyrik turned on them with a whoop and a laugh.

His fists drove them reeling back. Sweeping them off their feet, he tossed them aside as a man might throw away an empty fruit-skin. He scorned them, he insulted them with shouted words and knocked them senseless. And when he was done, he alone stood upon his feet.

"By the gods," he growled, staring around him at the ruined tavern, the limp and inert bodies. "Men have forgotten how to fight."

A horn called somewhere along the street and feet pounded in his direction. Kyrik picked up his sack and pushed his way to the door, opened it and stepped out into the sunlight. He let out a shout as he saw more watchmen, and behind them, soldiers of Devadonides' guard, attracted to the scene by the sounds of fierce fighting.

"One man?" roared a big watchman. "One man did all that damage?"

Kyrik bellowed with laughter and ran to meet him.

In later years, men told the story of that fight outside the ale house; they made poems about it, and songs, and so many were the cantos that men grew drunk over their wine-cups, toasting every one. For two hours the fight raged, and when it ended, when Kyrik sank at last to the ground and lay senseless because a bludgeon had caught him across the back of his head, more than forty men lay on the cobbled street around him.

One guardsman nursed a broken jaw, whispering, "That one isn't human. I'd swear he fights like a wounded bear, mad in his joy of battle."

Another growled, "He'll lose his happiness in the cells."

"Too bad, Lyssop. I'd like a friend like that when I go into battle. Gods! Can you imagine what he'd have done to us if he'd had a sword in his hand?"

Ten men carried Kyrik with his arms and legs strapped, and with his sack tied around his neck, through the streets on a shattered tabletop. They went through the older city, pausing not to heed the inquiries of curious men and women that thronged the walkways. By alleyways and narrow streets where the houses leaned together they went, and Kyrik noted that this part of the city which he had known so well, was not so much changed as he had feared. And so he smiled to secret thoughts.

To the ancient iron grille gate known as the Victory Arch they carried him, and along a court into a corridor dimly lighted all by oil lamps. To a room they brought him, propping him on his feet before an officer in a guard uniform who looked up at him with something like awe in his eyes.

"You're a big one," the officer muttered, turning from the sack he had been examining.

There was a silence. Then: "From whence come you, stranger?"

"From shipboard at the wharves of Pthesk. I'm a gypsy mercenary, I sell my sword to any man who needs a good one."

"So you can use that blade in your carryall can you, as well as you do your fists?"

Kyrik grinned. "Better. I have no equal in any land."

The officer raised his eyebrows. "Sa—ha! Is this truth or braggadocio?"

"Try me."

"Oh, I mean to. But not yet a while. I'll let your spirit simmer a bit in the darkness of a dungeon." He leaned across the tabletop confidentially. "If you can use that blade half so well as your tongue clacks about it, Devadonides might have a place for you in his guards corps."

"I'll take his gold. Why not?"

"For now, a cell to teach you not to drink too much. Take him away. I'll store your sack here until you sober up. Your personal property you can keep, we aren't robbers here."

He only promised that because if he became a guardsman, he might break a few heads to get it back, Kyrik told himself. He went meekly, as the sheep follows the bellwether. His furred boots moved along stone floors only slightly more worn than he had known them, ten centuries before. He sniffed the old, familiar odors—a bit of stale food, the stench of prisoners kept chained overlong, the damp wind that came from no man knew where, since it rose between the paving-stones of the floor where they had loosened.

His eyes gleamed when he saw where they took him: into the cells kept—in his time—for prisoners of repute, who might manage to pay a gold griff or two for good treatment. He waited patiently as the cell door was unlocked, endured the knife between his wrists that severed his binding ropes. He walked into the cell with a sigh. A guardsman growled, "You take this lightly enough. There are rats in these walls, and insects that bite to draw blood."

Kyrik said, "It's no worse than other places I've been. So treat me well, man, for I may be a companion in arms to you sooner than you know."

The man chuckled. "Aye, I'd enjoy having you at my side."

He put the lantern on the floor. "You can take it into your cell if you want light. You have a tinder box? Good. Then—pleasant dreams."

The man walked away. Kyrik took the lantern, blew out the flame. He was in almost total darkness, for the torchlight that illumined the corridors only touched this cell very faintly. Kyrik found the cot, lay back on it, put his hands behind his head.

He was right where he wanted to be. He slept until men came to wake him, one bearing a tray with food and drink on it, the other remaining in the corridor. They went away. Kyrik lit his lantern and devoured the stew and bread, drank from the leather jack that held cool ale. Then he lay back and slept some more.

Three men woke him, standing in the cell. One man said, "Time to come and test your swordsmanship, stranger. Kangor who is our captain would see the manner of your weapon-play Though I must warn you, he's in a rare mood since some of our fellows found him in a cottage trussed like a fowl for the roasting."

Kyrik smiled, yawned, rose upward. Once his feet were on the solid stone, his huge hands shot out to catch the heads of two of the guards. He rammed their foreheads together so hard the sound was like a shattering of a gourd dropped from a high place. The third man gaped, mouth open to shout. Kyrik caught his jaw with a fist. He lifted the lantern and locked the cell door behind him. Then he went swiftly, down one corridor and turning left at another until he came to a thick stone wall that was part of the castle foundations. He put down the lantern, placed his hands on the cold stone.

He fumbled a moment—a thousand years is a long time in the memory of a man—and then his fingers settled on a bit of masonry. He turned the stone, hard. It resisted his efforts and he thought that none had come this way in a long time. Indeed, he doubted whether Devadonides or any who served him knew of this secret way.

The mechanism functioned after a time, for Kyrik was a strong man and his muscles bulged with the effort he exerted. A part of the wall opened inward into blackness. Swiftly he stooped, caught up the lantern, stepped into that darkness. His hand pushed the wall-door shut. Kyrik lifted the lantern. There was thick dust on the stone floor, it showed no mark of any footprint. He grinned and moved forward confidently.

In a short time he came to a chamber enclosed on all sides by walls hung with draperies, molded and rotting now, but when he had known them rich and costly tapestries. An altar loomed before him, close to the farther wall, and behind the altar on a dais covered with once-red velvet long since turned to dusty nothingness, stood the statue of a naked woman.

Kyrik walked forward, lantern lifted. In the rays of that glow, the statue seemed alive. The woman was of a supernal loveliness, her high breasts arched outward invitingly, her smooth hips and dimpled belly, her slimly curved thighs and legs an invitation to venery. Her face was oval, framed by long golden hair that fell almost to the tips of her breasts. The full red mouth was pouting, the nostrils flared proudly. And the slanted gray eyes seemed to turn and study the barbarian as he advanced.

"Illis," he whispered. "It's been a long time." His hand set the lantern down, reached into his belt purse. Almost reverently he brought out the Lust-stone, placed it into a hollow in the dais before the statue. Kyrik stepped back, hardly breathing.

Slowly, very slowly, the pink tints of the statue flushed with life. It grew radiant, the rosy nipples stiffened, the firm thighs stirred. The hands that had been at rest beside the shapely hips lifted, went to her outer thighs. The red lips came apart in a smile.

"Kyrik of the Victories. It is good to see you again."

"You saw me in the forest glade with the gypsy girl."

Her laughter rang out as her palms lifted to her breasts, which she cupped. Tenderly she asked, "Is it the same thing, my worshiper?"

His grunt made her hold out her hands. He caught them, brought her down off the dais. His arms went about her nakedness, held her close as his mouth sought hers.

After a time she drew back. "Not many men can have the goddesses they worship come naked into their embrace, Kyrik. I hope you appreciate it."

He swung her up, carried her toward a marble bench. He sat down with her on his lap, kissed her lips lingeringly.

"I have often wondered what shape you are in the world from which you come, Illis."

The goddess gurgled laughter. "If I showed you, you might not be so attentive with your caresses. I was—jealous—of the way you took that gypsy girl."

"By doing that, I worshiped you."

"It's not the same thing, not at all!"

"Come, then. I'll make amends here and now." She sniffed, glancing about her. "The years have not been kind to my little fane. You must refurbish it, Kyrik. Make it beautiful as it was those years ago. Then. . ."

When his arms tightened, she put her fingers to his lips. Her smile vanished and her eyes grew sober. "Wait, Kyrik—wait. There are strange forces at work in Tantagol. It will not be as easy as you thought to push Devadonides off the throne that properly belongs to you. I must warn you."

It seemed to Kyrik that the room grew cold.

Chapter 5

He stared into those gray eyes.

"Wizardry?"

"What else?" Her smooth shoulders shrugged. "This sorcerer of Devadonides is powerful. Jokaline, his name is. He has placed many spells here and there about the castle. I learned of this from an imp that I caught trying to slip into my own world to do me harm."

She smiled cruelly. "He was sorry, afterward. But his tongue ran as does one of your mountain freshets, when he saw there was no hope. Now this I know: that if you think to become a guardsman, to come close to Devadonides and slay him—think no more of it. Those traps would close on you, you'd be whisked off into some region where even I might not help you. We goddesses, we demon lords and ladies, have only so much power, you know."

Kyrik scowled blackly. "I gave my word to aid Aryalla in her quest for vengeance. I won't abandon it."

Illis sighed, "I know. You're a proud man. I'll do what I can, naturally. Since you brought the Lust-stone back, I can come and go in your world as once I did, when the name of Kyrik was a power in the land. My worry is, that power may not be enough where the incantations of Jokaline are concerned."

"Then I'll put my trust in Bluefang." She pouted as might a human woman. "I will help, I will. But the way will not be as easy as you hoped. I should be with you at all times, you know. But how can I be? I can scarce walk through Tantagol City by your side. Besides," and here her mouth curved with hidden laughter, "you already have two girls at daggers' points over you."

He grunted. "If you had your sword. . ." He scowled at her. "Bluefang?"

"Yes, Bluefang. Go fetch it here." He rose, put her down on the cold marble bench. "I'll be back—very soon."

"Oh, Kyrik," she mocked. "So easily? Can you walk along the corridors of these dungeons and come and go as you please? Aren't you afraid of a dagger?"

"There are ways," he laughed. He walked across the room to a narrow door on one side of the chamber. This he opened, the rusted lock squealing protestingly, and stood a moment to stare back at her. His stare feasted on her nude beauty, which she knew well enough for she preened for him, flushing a little. Then he turned and closed the door and walked along a narrow way between thick stone walls until he came to a section of that wall which opened, after a time, to his fingers' grip.

He stepped into the outer corridor and walked confidently forward toward the guards room.

To his surprise, it was empty. His great sword was inside the sack on the floor. He reached for it, drew out his weapons belt, buckled that thick leather belt about his lean middle. A moment he stood, head bent in thought.

The guards officer would have become curious that the three men and their prisoner had not yet appeared. He might have gone to find them. In which case, they might be returning to this room in search of the escaped man. He picked up the sack and hurried back toward the entryway into the chamber.

He was ten feet away when the guards captain and the three men whom he had left within his cell turned the corner. Their eyes got big at sight of him, the guards captain shouted and drew his blade. They came in a rush, blades out and up. The men were raging, their eyes glinted fury and hate. The guards officer was more cautious, he remembered what Kyrik had told him about his swordplay. . Kyrik pulled Bluefang free of the scabbard. He caught their blades with a sweep of his own, said, "I don't wish to harm you. Go your way without me. I have—business—in these pits."

"Fool!" scoffed the officer, and thrust. Kyrik met his blade with a riposte, thrust so swiftly that his point was in and out of the man's shoulder before he could return his sword to its guard position. Almost in the same moment, the barbarian whirled on the others, drove them back and back. His point was always before their eyes, the edges slashing at exposed hands or when he bent, at their knees. They began to pant, and Kyrik mocked them. "If I was your officer, I'd see you spent less time swilling ale and wenching and more in practicing your swordplay. You three aren't fit to guard a dung-heap!"

One man he felled by bringing the flat of his blade across his skull.

A second he wounded with a sideways slash at his arm that he laid open to the bone. The third would have turned and fled, but Kyrik was too close behind him. His left arm darted out, he caught the man and drove his head against the closest stone wall. The man sank in a heap.

Kyrik turned on the wounded man who clutched his gashed arm and glared at him. "I am sorry, friend, but—" His fist hammered into the man's face.

The way was clear, now. No man could see how he touched the stone wall and the manner of its opening. The four men lay unconscious on the stone floor. Kyrik moved into the narrow opening, closed it.

He hastened back toward Illis in her worshiping chamber. She was moving about the room, graceful, lissome, and once more Kyrik wondered at her shape and form in those demon lands that called her mistress. She laughed at sight of him and his bloody sword and ran to him on bare feet.

Her fingertips touched the bloody blade, wiped it clean. As might a child, she put that finger to her mouth, licked off the blood. Her blonde eyebrows rose questioningly.

"Do I shock you, Kyrik darling? Is my thirst for blood so baffling to your human mind?"

His wide shoulders lifted, fell. "There are night creatures who need blood for life. To you it's a tasty thing. Who am I to condemn your demon ways?"

Her palm patted his jaw. "Nice Kyrik. You always say the right thing. But come, put your sword upon my altar."

He placed it where she said, watched as she bent to put her hands upon its hilt. A moment she stood thus, and Kyrik held his breath. Then her naked body shimmered, faded, grew nebulous. He cried out in his surprise, started forward. Yet he did not touch her, he had learned a long time ago to humor the whims of this demon-woman whom his family had worshiped since the days his people had built Tantagol City.

Then, Illis was gone. And, in her place—Kyrik stared down at his sword-hilt about which was now entwined a golden, glittering serpent. It was wrapped about the hilt, the quillions. His hand wrapped fingers about that snake-sheathed grip. The snake was warm, as female flesh is warm, and a sense of life came to his hand where he held it.

"I shall be with you, this way," a voice whispered in his head.

He grinned at the glittering eyes of the golden serpent. "And be an embarrassment to me when I make love to the gypsy girl, next time."

"I shall bite her, Kyrik"

"Na, na. I only take her to worship you." The snake glared at him. He sheathed the sword, doffed his gypsy clothes, donned his habergeon and mail shirt, his war-boots Then he went out into the corridor through the first stone wall so that he stepped into a part of the pits on the far side of that hall where the guards lay unconscious. As he moved along the tunnel, he thought back on his memories of the dungeons, he knew little passageways that he felt sure were not used in these days of that first Devadonides' descendant.

He saw no one. There were few guards stationed in the pits, he realized. What was there in these cold, dank prisons to require a guard? The few prisoners who waited in their cells were helpless, half-starved men. At times he trotted, he went up worn stone steps that had been old when he had borne the golden scepter of Tantagol in his hand. In time he came to a street door, bolted.

With his dagger-point he picked the lock, stepped into sunlight. He sauntered casually, being to any casual viewer nothing but a sell-sword out of employment. And as he went, he wondered about Aryalla and where she might be.

"You can help me, Illis," he breathed. "Find the sorceress."

"At least, you haven't had her yet. Wait Kyrik walked while Illis quested in her demoniac way. He entered a tavern, downed slices of meat and bread and cheese, swallowed two tankards of ale. He made no disturbance, he stayed in the darker shadows, for he sought only anonymity here, and despite his size and appearance, few did more than glance at him.

And then: "Hurry, Kyrik The woman is in danger."

"Where away?" He felt something brush his mind. He turned, went where that subtle pull took him, along wide thoroughfares and mean, narrow streets, until he came to a row of houses black with age. Into one of these he turned, put hand to doorknob, turned it and went into a hallway hung with cheeses. A narrow stair led upward to the second floor. Kyrik took the stairs, went where the snake-thoughts brought him, to a blue door warped with years. His knuckles rapped.

Something stirred inside the room. "It's Kyrik," he breathed, and the door opened. Aryalla stared at him with huge black eyes, half fearfully. She reached out, caught his arm, dragged him into the tiny room. There was the smell of Frankonian incense in the air, the acrid bite of magic.

"You've been making spells," he said. "I had to find you! Where in the name of the gods have you been?"

"In gaol, as I told you." Her face was almost ludicrous in surprise. "In Devadonides' prison cells? And you walk out a free man?"

"I cracked a skull or two. But I wanted to let you know we must leave Tantagol City."

Suspicion touched her eyes. "You've given up your quest for vengeance?"

"We're helpless against Devadonides while he sits inside his castle. It's set with demoniac traps. How many, I can't guess. But they're there."

"How can you know this?"

"Illis told me. The goddess I worship for her beauty."

"A goddess—pah She's helpless in Tantagol." It seemed to Kyrik that a snake hissed inside his head.

Aryalla gave him a sly glance. "Besides, Illis is dead, except when you call her name. And I don't think she's as lovely as you make her out to be."

Now Kyrik knew a snake hissed. "Just the same, I know it. I also know something else, that Jokaline will trace out the remnants of that spell you used to try and find me. Not much goes on in Tantagol City that the wizard doesn't learn, and tell Devadonides. So gather up your things, and let's be on our way."

"Where? Where is there a better place for us than here?"

"Illis! Will you argue with me?" Aryalla turned to lift up her cloak and the little coffer in which she carried certain necessities of her trade. But already it was too late. The heavy feet coming up the worn staircase swung Kyrik around. He growled low in his throat, put a

64

hand on his serpent-twined hilt and drew his sword. It came into the light, long and bright, the blued blade glittering with rune-work

"Get behind me," he told Aryalla. "Be rid of her, Kyrik darling." He ignored the serpent voice, he lifted the sorceress in an arm and carried her toward a window. He glanced out and up. There were eaves overhanging the wall and window: alone and with time he might have made his escape. The door burst inward. Mailed men came into the room. At sight of Kyrik when they had been expecting only a woman, they drew their weapons.

"Surrender," commanded the captain. Kyrik charged. Bluefang swung in his hand as though alive, he slashed at faces and arms, he parried steel. His bull rush carried him upon and past the soldiers before they realized that he meant to fight. Three were down, but now the other were cutting at him and he dodged, ducked beneath the swing of sword-blades, to make his way toward the narrow door. His back to that opening, he fought as he had been wont to fight against his foes a thousand years before. And the human magic that was in his sword-hand had not deserted him. Two more men fell before the others drew back, gaping at him. Kyrik spared them no more than a swift glance before he turned his back and yanking at Aryalla, fled down the hall. Swiftly he went, with his war-boots barely touching the planks, then plunged down the stairs at breakneck speed.

Aryalla slipped and stumbled; she would have fallen but for his hand that kept her upright. They plunged out into the street; above their heads the guards captain was bellowing, shouting."

"Stop that man! Stop him or die in his place!"

They ran, bent over and heeding not whether their feet splashed into slop that made little splotches on the cobblestones. Aryalla was whimpering, panting, able to run only because the barbarian was dragging her along.

"Let her go," whispered Illis. "You'll never make it with her as an anchor to your feet."

He disregarded the serpent voice, he owed a dept to the sorceress, a debt he meant to pay. He also had the feeling that he might have need of her necromantic powers if ever he were to take his place on the throne that belonged to him. And so Kyrik rumbled curses in his throat as his war-boots barely skimmed the cobblestones, while he dragged Aryalla sobbing in his wake.

The captain's shouts echoed overhead. In answer to those cries, men began to tumble from the taverns, moving out of wine-shops and alehouses to stare with big eyes as they saw the huge barbarian careening down on them with the sorceress racing to keep up. One or two men tried to stop him, they were battered aside as though they were no more than children. Kyrik disdained to use his sword on them.

But the streets were aroused. Men shouted, women screamed. Though life under Devadonides was none so pleasant that they wanted to die, still these people must cover themselves against reprisals, and so a hubbub went at his heels as he fled through the narrow streets and alleyways of the Old City. He knew this section well. The leather gambeson he wore under his shirt of fine mesh had been softened at the tannery he could see in the next block, he had come with his war captains to quench battle—fevered thirsts in an alehouse past which he was racing, long ago. A broken culvert he saw in the next block once had carried water into the palace.

No man knew him now, even his name was almost forgotten in this day and age. To these onlookers he was no more than a wandering sell-sword who dared to steal a woman and was making off with her. A few greedy ones might covet his great sword with the golden serpent twined about its handle, but Kyrik had a rough and ready look; he gave the impression that he knew how to use that blade, and would, were any to be so stupid as to try and intercept him. They would leave that to the soldiers.

And the soldiers were coming. As he dove with Aryalla into a cul-de-sac, Kyrik could hear their war-horns blowing, the cries of their officers striving to make order out of the chaos of a street chase.

Lookouts were being posted, fast runners were being dispatched down one street and then another to locate him.

"We're going to have to fight," he panted. "With—what?"

"My sword and your sorcery, girl." He swung her sideways off her feet so that her spine bumped into a cracked wooden door. "By Illis! You're a sorceress! Can't you think of some incantation that will hide us from the men who seek us?"

Aryalla licked her lips. "I—I can make conjurations—yes! But I need time!"

Kyrik grinned coldly. "Not even a simple spell, like drawing darkness upon the city and giving us the eyes to see through it?"

"Of course," she exclaimed indignantly. "The druidical priests of distant Albiona can do such tricks. I can do more."

"Then do it, woman. Or—too late!" Three warriors rounded the corner at the far end of the street. They saw Kyrik, bellowed, ran for him with naked swords. The barbarian cursed, yanked out Bluefang and went to meet them. Steel rang, drew sparks. Kyrik fought on the defensive, he had no wish to wound these men or slay them. And so he battled with blurring blade, seeking opportunities only to bring the flat of his blade down upon their skulls. One man fell, and then another. The third man turned and fled.

"He'll be back," groused Kyrik, "with others." His hand yanked Aryalla from the doorway, made her run as he ran, lightly and conserving energy. This was a mean section of the Old City, it was its most ancient part. Wandering tribesmen had settled here centuries before Kyrik had been born, driven from the south-lands by hordes of little dark men who fought like lunatics with short bows from horseback, and who worshiped a god called Alyut. Here had settled the Scyts, the Vandars, the Gotts; here had they lived in peace, out of necessity, their men and women mating and forming one mixture of races. They were barbarians, blonde and golden haired, for the most part, with white skins that tanned darkly in the sun of Tantagol. Their greatest warriors were their chiefs, and the chiefs met when their supreme chieftain died, to select a new ruler. Until the advent of Kyrik's own grandfather, Kornak, that is, who led his armies east and west, north and south, and captured a great territory; Kornak then declared that his son and his son's son should be kings in Tantagol even when he died.

Now Kyrik was the last of his line. Ah, but not the least of that long heritage of warriors, chieftains and kings. In his veins was the blood of Kornak, of Erikin, of Kyron. Great warriors, these, and mighty chiefs. He would not be taken by Devadonides' mercenaries! Better to dare death itself.

Kyrik knew where death lay waiting for him and the woman who stumbled in weariness and fell against him from time to time as she staggered. In the middle of the Old City, which his ancestors had ruled, was the Well of Emptiness, a great hole in the ground-made by an extinct geyser, the wise men used to say—that had no bottom. He would make his last stand there, with the well-stones at his back and the woman in the crook of an arm. If his sword failed to cut a way to safety for them, he would leap into that well with Aryalla.

He came at last to the thoroughfare that stretched straight ahead toward the circle of stones that was the well. In front of him were armed mercenaries in the black and gold livery of Tantagol. They saw him, they shouted, they came with their swords and battleaxes glinting in the sunlight. Kyrik ran to meet them, a hand on Aryalla's wrist.

Bluefang flashed, darted. Kyrik could spare no time for the niceties of his swordplay. He must beat a path toward that well, turn his back to it and fight as he had never fought before. And so men went down before his point and edges, they fell to lie unmoving as his steel clove a way between them.

Aryalla sobbed at his side, teeth to her knuckles. Three men fell, then five, and the way was clear. Kyrik backhanded a blow at an officer, saw his steel drive into his throat, yanked his sword clear and bent to catch up the sorceress. As though she were a child, he bore her across those cobblestones and to the Well of Emptiness. Then he sat her on the wide rim and turned once more to face his foes.

They came at him, they were brave men who earned the silver rhodanthes that Devadonides paid them. They were veterans of his battles, they had never before faced a single swordsman who could hold off so many of their number. They disregarded wounds to hurl themselves at him, they pressed forward in their weight of numbers. And they died.

Like a shuttle was the blade of Kyrik as he drove it left and right, paused to parry and thrust. Untiring was his thickly thewed arm that wielded that heavy length of blue steel as though it were no more than a wooden stake. His edge bit, his point drove home, until the blade called Bluefang was wet with dripping blood. More men came running. War-horns sounded.

"By Illis!" Kyrik rasped. "They bring a regiment!"

He fought them as long as he could, but they came behind him onto the rim of the well, and he could not defend himself against swordpoints at his back. For a little while he fought on the defensive, contenting himself with parrying to stay alive, but he knew that sooner or later, a blade would penetrate that marvelous defense, he would be wounded and lose blood. After a bitter exchange of sword-strokes, the warriors drew back to breathe hard and stare at Kyrik in something akin to awe.

"By the gods, fellow," said one, "Tantagol has never seen such blade-work Why don't you give yourself up and come with us?"

"We'd welcome a man like you." Kyrik grinned at them, as one warrior to another. "Tell Devadonides I've sworn to push him off his throne. Tell him my name is—Kyrik of the Victories!"

He whirled and leaped, coming down on top of the well rim. His arm shot out, closed about Aryalla. For a moment he held her soft and yielding against him, listening to her cry out in terror. He sheathed his sword. Then he leaped into the well.

Chapter 6

There is no bottom to the Well of Emptiness.

For ages, men have amused themselves by dropping pebbles down it, straining ears to hear the plop of stone in water. And there has never been a man who claimed to hear that sound. Wise men said that there was no bottom to this well, that it went down into the very bowels of the planet, that there was only molten magma there to catch and melt the bones of any man who fell into it. They said also that a man who leaped into the well might die before he reached that molten matter.

Kyrik remembered all this as he leaped. There was black nothingness below him, the wind whistling in his ears as he and Aryalla plummeted downward. He lifted his head to stare at the receding circle of stone that was the well itself. He saw amazed faces, astounded faces. Then they were gone as they fell and fell until the hole closed and there was nothing about them but solid blackness. They went down feet first, so swiftly that they could not breathe.

Kyrik understood now what the wise men meant when they said a man might die before he touched the molten magma far below. His lungs were straining, he felt the woman's soft weight about him as she fainted.

And then—

Cold water drank them in.

They went down and down into that water, until Kyrik thought he was going to die for lack of air. He strained, he lashed out at these flowing waters with his feet, he fought to rise upward. The current aided him when he was deep within it. It bubbled and ran through these dark caverns, it lifted him and Aryalla, it spewed them from it out upon its surface. And then it carried them along, swirling and tossed as though they were no more than wood chips, where it pleased, now it pleased. Arms tightened about his neck.

"Are we dead?" a voice whispered. "Are we in Haderos, where men say their spirits go when they die?"

"We're in a river," he growled. "And save your breath, you may need it."

Occasionally the current carried them against stone walls, bumping them badly, but Kyrik fought free of them, and swam to stay in the middle of the river. The air was fresh, which buoyed his spirits, a wind blew steadily through these black caves, and from time to time he caught the scent of growing things.

"We'll come out of it sometime," he told the woman. "Smell those wildflowers? The meadow grass? Neither of those can grow in here, without the sun."

The water was cold as glacial ice; it numbed their bodies and their muscles, so that after a time, even mighty Kyrik sagged and let the water carry him down under the surface, yielding to that mental indifference that the coldness put in him. Yet when he would have sunk never to rise, it was Aryalla who woke him, nails sinking into his flesh.

"Kyrik—look! Up ahead. . ." He opened numbed eyelids, saw a faint circle of bright light. And now came hope to bolster his spirits, so that he struck out, swimming strongly against the chill in his body. Sunlight up ahead meant an end to these damply dripping stone walls, to this blackness shrouding them. Sunlight meant warmth and life.

They came out of the tunneled cavern, bobbing on the waters. Kyrik saw green fields and trees, saw mountains in the distance, purple with haze. He struck out for shore and now Aryalla no longer clung to him, fearing to lose contact; seeing that grassy bank, she too began to swim. They came onto the land, crawling there. Kyrik sank onto his belly, lay panting. A desperate tiredness was in his every muscle, he wanted nothing more than to rest here. The sun beat down on him, drying and warming him; he let his eyes close. Out of long habit his hand went to his sword hilt, felt the golden snake and the hilt; he was content.

Aryalla had lost her cloak and coffer of magical materials in the river currents, she stood now, shivering slightly to her wetness, in a thin garment of Inisfalian silk that lay plastered to her flesh. She stared around her at low hills, at rolling meadows.

"Where are we, Kyrik?" she wondered. He rolled onto his back, stared at the blue sky and the clouds scudding past. "Beyond the city, along a stretch of land said by men who should know, to be haunted by devils. Even when I was king in Tantagol, men came not to this land, it was shunned."

He sat up, stared where the woman looked. He grunted. "A fair land, it is. Now why is it haunted, I wonder—and by whom?"

Kyrik came to his feet, towering above the woman. He growled, loosed the sword in its scabbard. "I've a mind to find out," he rumbled.

Aryalla gave him a horrified glance. "Aren't we in enough trouble? After what we've been through, I need to rest."

He grinned at her, knowing her to be unconscious of the fact that the thin silk tunic, that came to the middle of her thighs, showed her almost naked. The wetness made the sheer stuff cling, it revealed the fullness of her breasts, her curving hips, the gentle mounds of belly. When she saw the way he stared, she flushed, then raised her chin defiantly. "I'm no round-heels to be tossed on the grass and enjoyed the way you did Myrnis!"

Kyrik laughed, caught her by a bare arm, swung her in against him. He knew the softness of her body, its attraction. His green eyes stared down into her angry face.

"Woman, if I wished, I could have you now, and well you know it. You want me, it's there in your black eyes—" The serpent on his sword hissed. "— but I have other things to do."

He released her, caught the hand she swung at his face. "Na, na. Be not offended. I find you good to look upon. It's just that the sun is setting and a hunger makes my belly empty."

She scowled at him, but Kyrik knew she was mollified. No woman likes to be thought unattractive. She rubbed her arm where his fingers had vised, and stared off across the meadows.

"There is danger, Kyrik!" He heard that hissing voice, stared around him. "Over the nearer hill."

"Come," he said to Aryalla and began his walk. They moved across the meadow-land, set their feet on pine needles and the tiny flowers of the woodlands floor as they began their climb up the hill. Aryalla walked at his heels, quietly in her sandals, and his own war-boots made little sound on the soft loam forest floor. When they came to the crown of the hill, they found themselves looking at a long valley, and in the center of it, framed by trees planted to make a park about its white marble walls, was a small temple. Its pillars glinted red in the sunlight, its dome was of a pearly hue.

Aryalla whimpered, "It's an evil place." Kyrik turned his head to stare down at her. "Now how can you know that, woman? It's beautiful. I never knew it existed."

"My powers make me—sensitive."

"Let's go find out how right you are." The golden serpent hissed, "She's right. There is much danger in that ancient fane. I feel it too—"

Stubbornly, Kyrik went on walking. An anger was inside him, he felt himself to have played a poor role in what had taken place, this far in his new-found life. He had been hounded, attacked, made to run, forced to flee ignominiously, like some ragged cut-purse And he—a king. He needed something on which to vent his spleens.

The nearer they came to the temple, the more curious Kyrik became. There were no priests about, no worshipers

He came up onto the portico, passed between the pillars. The sorceress hung back, whimpering. The woman he ignored, went through the open doorway into a dim quiet.

"Isthinissis dwells here!" He caught the shock in that mental voice that was Illis, almost felt her shudder. Kyrik paused. Isthinissis was a fable, no more. In his time, it had been the name of a serpent god of these people from the south-lands, dreaded even by its worshipers To his barbaric people, it was an unspeakable abomination. The Lilthians had fed living women to it, he recalled.

"Shall I go back?" he wondered. "Too late. It comes The temple was round, comprising only one large chamber. In the geometrical center of its floor stood a raised stone dais, smooth and gleaming, with stone steps, railed, leading to the platform itself which rimmed a black hole. It reminded Kyrik of the Well of Emptiness. Could it be that this was the exit to a burrow in which dwelt some strange serpent being? He put a hand to Bluefang, drew the blued blade. The golden serpent was warm to his touch, like woman-flesh. Kyrik could hear a slithery rasping far down in the bowels of the ground. The temple shook slightly, as though a quake were moving it.

"What comes, Illis?"

"The demon god, Isthinissis!"

"Is there any way to kill it?"

"I know not! I know not Kyrik grinned coldly. Inside that tunnel-way, the demon god could not use its full strength. His only hope lay in meeting it with cold steel before it could emerge from that round opening. He went up the smooth stone stairway, three treads at a time, and stepped to the rim of the hole.

He could hear it coming, now. It hissed, it made leathery sounds where it scraped the walls of its underground corridor. A fetid odor came out, to make Kyrik grimace and turn aside his head.

Then he saw a gleaming redness, rising slowly. He had no way of knowing how long, how monstrous was the entire being, all he had eyes for was that pulsing redness that glowed faintly, radiating scarlet beams. To Kyrik, it seemed that the red thing was a membranous sac that dimmed and shone from moment to moment. He waited as the thing came higher, closer, Bluefang lifted in his hand. Up it came, toward the rim. And Kyrik leaned down, thrust with the blued blade. Isthinissis bellowed, and his bellow shook the temple.

As his sword sank into that red membrane to its hilt, gore spouted. It was not human blood, it was ichor that stank, that stung where its drops touched Kyrik's sword-hand and arm. He growled curses, but kept his grip on the sword. He raised it, slashed again and yet again. Now the entire temple was shaking, as it might to a severe quake. The barbarian never ceased his efforts, he stabbed and cut as though his very life depended on it; which it might, he told himself wryly.

"It—retreats, Kyrik!" The thing was sliding back the way it had come, wounded. Its moans were hollow roars magnified by the walls of the burrow. The redness stank, it dripped along the walls of that narrow passageway, dimly lighting it.

"The wickedness I felt is—fading! I think you slew it, Kyrik! And I catch its thoughts, but only vaguely. It whispers in its terror, it thinks of—of Devadonides. I wonder—why?"

"Maybe Devadonides made it serve him."

"Yes. Yes, I think that is so. Wait, don't speak again."

For long moments Kyrik stood at the rim of the platform, waiting. The demon was long since gone, it had fled back into whatever labyrinthine ways it traveled, far below the surface of the land. Perhaps those ways led to the south-lands, there might be other openings there, if the Lilthians who occupied those warmer climes worshiped it.

"It huddles far below. It—dies. And dying, it remembers the days of its youth, those eons ago when it came into being, when it was worshiped as a god. It recalls Devadonides, how that first ancestor of the present king used its powers to put that spell on you, Kyrik, that changed you into a statue!"

The barbarian grinned. "You paid it back with—death. For it dies, with its membrane pierced. It will lie there and rot, and perhaps in its death throes it will shake the ground and the temple will fall. Let's get out of it."

Kyrik needed no second urging. He cleansed the blade of Bluefang on a bit of drapery, ran for the temple entrance. As he did so, he could feel the floor heaving underfoot, heard bits of marble dislodged from place, falling to the tiled floor. He came out into the sunlight with the marble pillars of the fane buckling under the pressure of the domed temple roof and the shaking of the ground. Aryalla was before him at a little distance, a hand to her mouth, black eyes enormous in her terror, backing away.

"What—is it?" she cried out. "Isthinissis dies," he shouted, and leaped off the stone steps, hearing the falling of masonry, the crumbling of ancient columns and the last awful crash of domed ceiling to the tiled floor. He sprinted, ran for the sorceress, swept her up in an arm and dove for the ground that was rising, falling as might a sea wave. It lifted the man and woman, bouncing them. They could hear, dimly and from far away, the death wails of the dying thing even as they felt its death throes through the buckling ground. Aryalla moaned.

After a time, the creature died, the ground subsided. The temple lay wrecked, pillars tumbled inward, the domed roof a mere mass of shattered shards.

He told her of the thing, the manner of its slaying, but he did not mention the fact that Illis had spoken to his mind of what she had learned from its dying brain. The sorceress shivered, for with the setting of the sun, the wind was colder.

Kyrik saw this, said, "I'll make a fire." Dry boughs and branches, little dry stalks of dead underbrush he gathered together and with his tinder box made a tiny flame that became a fire. They sat about it, staring into it, the woman close to him so that she rested her side against the man.

"I wish we had some food," she murmured.

"Tomorrow," he promised. After a time they slept, huddled together for warmth. The night was cold in this wilderness, from time to time Kyrik rose to put more wood on the flames. When he did this, his eyes rested on the woman so nearly naked who slept beside him. He hungered for her flesh, he put a hand toward her hip, but instead of caressing it, he merely drew her closer and into his arms for mutual warmth.

They woke in the morning to a touch of steel at their throats. Kyrik let his eyes study the bearded man with the spear who glared down at him. He was clad in furs, a rusted mail shirt, and he wore sword and dagger at his hip. With him were five other ragged men, outlaws all by the look of them.

Kyrik said, "We're no threat to you." The bearded man growled, "Any who pass through these lands of Almorak are a threat. How do I know you aren't spies sent by Devadonides?"

Kyrik laughed. "You too? I fled from his soldiers by leaping down the Well of Emptiness."

The spear-point pressed until it drew a drop of blood. "You lie. That well has no bottom."

"We fell into the river. It's why we're alive."

"And soon to die!" Kyrik asked, "What? And after what I did for you?"

"And what have you done for Almorak?" The barbarian hesitated. He had no way of knowing whether these ragged men had worshiped Isthinissis, but he believed they did not, they hadn't the look of religious fanatics about them.

He said, "I slew the thing in the temple. Didn't it prey on your people?"

Almorak looked at him a long time. He said, "If you did that, you are my friend. Aye, it snatches a man or two and a woman when it prowls these lands —that's why none but us outlaws will live here. Devadonides can't send an army—even his soldiers won't come into these haunted hills. How can I know if what you say is true?"

"Send a man to look at the temple. It's in ruins."

"No man of mine will go down into the valley."

"Then let the woman and I go first, and you follow. If the monster comes out to feed, it will snatch us first."

Almorak gestured, Kyrik and Aryalla rose to their feet. They walked side by side up a hill and down it, to the ridge of the next. The valley lay before them, the white marbled fane in shattered ruins.

The outlaw chief cursed. His hairy hand clapped Kyrik on the shoulder. "By the gods, man. I don't know how you did it, I won't ask. But you've earned my friendship for what it's worth."

Kyrik let his eyes study the chief and his men. They were hardy fellows, big-boned and raw-skinned They looked to be hard fighting men. And he needed an army, if he were ever going to overthrow Devadonides.

He said suddenly, "How many do you number?"

"A thousand, a few more. Many of our men are in Devadonides' dungeons. That offal wars on us, sends men into the hills after us when we raid the caravans that come from Arazalla and Karalon. They don't come deep into these hills but occasionally they catch a few of us on the roads."

Kyrik growled, "Feed me and the woman. I've a plan to free those men of yours, if I can enlist you and your outlaws in my fight against Devadonides."

Almorak stared at him as though he were mad. "Fight Devadonides? We outlaws? You lay too long in moonlight." He grinned, showing big teeth. "At least, I like your nerve. Come, if you want to eat."

They went by hill-walks to a ridge where a few tents showed between the trees. Here were women and a few children, quietly standing and staring as they came forward. Four men bore a spear-haft that held a dead deer, tied by its hooves above the shaft; for Almorak and his men had gone hunting early.

Aryalla sat with Kyrik as they ate and drank ale, and chewed on black bread and cheese. When they were done eating, Kyrik explained his plans. He would go into Tantagol as a beggar, and lead out the imprisoned outlaws who waited to die by whatever tortures Devadonides' executioners could think up. He would bring them to the hills where they would be free.

"In return, we raid the caravans together. From Arazalla come the special herbs and spices Aryalla needs to work her magicks."

The outlaws looked at the sorceress, made signs in the air to protect themselves from her black eyes. Kyrik grinned, putting a hand on her shoulder and shaking it.

"She makes magic for us, to dethrone Devadonides. She won't harm you. But we must have magic on our side because Jokaline works his spells in favor of the king."

Almorak leaned forward. "You did yourself a good turn when you slew Isthinissis. Devadonides counts on him for much help in those necromancies of Jokaline."

Kyrik remembered what Illis had whispered to his mind in the temple. He asked in surprise, "How can a big snake—or whatever Isthinissis was—help Jokaline the wizard?"

"He wasn't just a snake. That was only his earthly form. He is a demon god, in his own world. Or so I've heard it said. But it was as a reptile that he could work the wonders Jokaline asked of him. His snake body served as some sort of—of gateway through which his demonic powers could pass. Without that body, he isn't as strong as he was."

Kyrik grunted, getting to his feet. "Give me some old clothes, Almorak. I would be a beggar, going into Tantagol City once more."

They found old garments to cover his chain-mail shirt and his fur kilt, bits of bagging to wrap about his war-booted feet. He wore a big cloak, patched a hundred times, and someone thrust a beggar's bowl into his hand, with a staff on which to lean. Kyrik bent his body so that he seemed half his height, and walked by dragging a leg behind him. Almorak grinned and nodded. "You'll do. Nobody will suspect you for a warrior. Can you keep that sword of yours out of sight?"

"I'll strap it to my leg so my leg won't bend, and keep the cloak about it. I'll beg for alms in the old city which I know better than the new."

Almorak looked doubtful. "You can get into the dungeons without anyone seeing you? And bring my men out again?"

"Tomorrow, watch the roads for us." Kyrik chuckled. "We may be in a hurry, so bring your bows to shaft down any who might be chasing us."

He set out with the sun not yet risen to its full, and toward the end of the day when the shadows were longest, he sighted the walls of Tantagol City. It would not do to be caught outside the city walls when they were closed for the night so Kyrik hurried as best he might against the setting sun, and was not above begging a ride off a farm cart that was traveling into the city to bring hides for the morrow's selling.

He begged his way along the street, crying out that he was a soldier disabled in many battles, that he had not eaten since yesterday, and not drunk ale for a full week. People passed him by without opening their purses, but a drunken man threw him a silver rhodanthe and a soldier tossed him a few coppers. He shook his wooden bowl, he limped along dragging his leg. From a street-stall he bought bread and cheese and a little meat, with a small wine-skin. He crouched against the base of a stone building in the poorer quarter of the Old City, eating, and drinking the wine. The passersby gave him no notice, except for a man or two who booted his shrouded, bent form. When this happened, Kyrik whimpered and crawled deeper into the shadows; none saw the flare of anger in his green eyes.

At last the moon was high in the sky, and Kyrik seemingly dozed, nodding from time to time, propped against the wall. There were less and less people in the streets, soon there were none. And now Kyrik rose and unstrapped his sword from his leg, and ran. He went swiftly, keeping always to the darker side of the street and out of the moonlight, until he came to an old culvert that had brought water into the city in the days when he had been a boy. He had seen this culvert when he and Aryalla had fled from the soldiers of the king, and remembered it.

He went along that culvert, wondering if it had been blocked up, wondering if those drains that had brought water to the city reservoirs a thousand years ago, had been walled up. If they had, he could never get into the dungeons. He ran through the darkness of the culvert and when he had gone far enough, he halted and began to feel along the curving culvert wall to his right as he walked. His hand felt emptiness, his heart lurched. "By Illis! It's still here, after all the years." He ran now, feeling confident.

He knew these waterways, he had seen to their refurbishing when he had been king in Tantagol. They led under the city houses; they fed into the palace and the dungeons, into army barracks and certain old fountains that now were dry. Instead of . these antiquated waterways, the city had fine new aqueducts to the north.

A flight of stone steps, very cramped, very narrow, went upward to the roof. Kyrik mounted them, fumbled at the worn wooden covering above them. His muscles tensed, the round cover rose. He stared along a torch-lit floor. He was in the lower dungeons. He came out of the culvert, replaced the cover. On the burlap wrappings about his warboots he made no sound as he moved along the dungeon corridors. Not until he heard men snoring or turning fitfully in sleep behind barred doors did he pause. Softly he called, "Almorak sent me." Many times he spoke that name before a snore choked off and a man breathed, "Who speaks the name of the outlaw chief?"

"A friend of Almorak's who sent me here to free you.

There was soft movement in the pits' darkness. "By the old gods. I have to believe you, because I can't understand why our jailers would bother to play such a trick—if it is a trick."

"No trick. Who has your keys?"

"The night gaoler. He'll be in his little cubicle, dead drunk as he always is. And, friend—if you can, bring his wine-skin if there's even a swallow left in it. It's been weeks since I tasted anything to drink but the foul water Devadonides provides for those about to die."

Kyrik chuckled, moved away. Like a shadow he passed along corridors, crossed intersections, until he found himself guided by a spray of light from an open door. To the door he went, peered inside. A man lay with his head on his crossed arms that were stretched out upon a tabletop. A half-full wine-skin lay at his elbow, and from time to time the man snored faintly. Kyrik grinned. Devadonides' jailers had an easy life. He drew his dagger, stepped into the room. He meant to kill the man to keep him silent, but at the last moment, hammered his head with the hilt pommel, instead.

He sheathed his dagger, grabbed up the wine-sack, lifted down all the key-rings on the wooden rack. Then he sped back along the way he had come. There were others awake and at their bars when he returned. They spoke in whispers at sight of him, they stared as he freed one man and then another. Kyrik handed the wine-skin to the first man who had spoken to him.

He asked, "Which of these are Almorak's men?"

"Two hundred and a few. But why not free them all?"

"Will they sound an alarm?" Soft laughter running from many throats was his answer. He handed out the keys, watched as ragged man after ragged man went to free their fellows. They made a great throng, it was Devadonides' delight to round up homeless men from the streets and use them in the arena to amuse himself and his nobles.

"You have garments, such as they are," said Kyrik. "Cling by them to the man in front of you. I go first, for I know the way."

They went single file, and there were so many it was a long time since all of them must go down the stone steps into the culvert and await his coming. Kyrik moved last down those steps, replacing the cover. In case of a pursuit, he did not want to give his enemies any more help than need be.

Through the culvert and out into the moonlight they went, to sniff at clean air and stare at the moons and the clouds high overhead. On their faces was a new hope, the disbelief of men snatched suddenly and unexpectedly from death.

"How do we get out of the city?" asked a voice. Kyrik grinned. "Through the other end of the culvert. It was broken here, but beyond those houses it should begin again. It dips down under the walls, and appears again outside them. Come!"

They made good time, they were quiet, only the shuffle of their feet told where they walked. Close to the city wall, Kyrik found again the culvert, disappeared inside it, the others following after. In time, they emerged from the earthenware tunnel, came out into the moonlight at the edge of a wood. Here Kyrik halted and drew them around him.

"We go to join Almorak, who offers fighting and good loot. But he and I offer something more. A chance to bring Devadonides down from his throne." Their howls of delight told him they were his men. Fists were shaken, tormented bodies quivered with the need for vengeance.

"His men took my wife. When I fought, they threw me into a cell. I go with you."

"My brother they slew!"

"My father died on the rack!" They hated with a fury that showed itself in contorted faces and hate-filled eyes. Life meant little to these lost men, but they would sell what they owned with pleasure, if it meant the end of the Tantagol tyrant.

Kyrik led them through the wood and they came upon the outlaw camp at sunrise. They were welcomed and fed, given ale to drink. Almorak came and walked among them, greeting his old comrades in arms, marveling that Kyrik had done what he promised.

"I thought you were a dead man when you walked away from here. Your woman's been worried, too." His head jerked toward Aryalla who stood staring at Kyrik with big eyes. "Now we've got them back, what do we do with them?"

"Raid the caravans." Almorak scowled. "The caravans from Arazalla are well guarded. Men-at-arms patrol the line on horseback. It won't be easy." He shook his bearded head. "We usually only raid the smaller columns, those with poor merchants who can't afford to hire too many guards."

Kyrik chuckled, "I have a way." He went to Aryalla, caught her by an arm. "In Tantagol City, you said you could raise a darkness, if you had time."

"And so I can, Kyrik. What would you?" He told her and she listened, and smiled, and gave a soft laugh. "Aye, it may work. I'll do what needs to be done. I'll need certain herbs, though."

Almorak sent the women to gather those herbs. Then Kyrik walked with him through the camp, bringing the outlaws to their feet. Kyrik took them to a high ridge that overlooked the Tantagol road.

"Post lookouts to tell us when a rich caravan comes," he said to Almorak. "When it's been sighted, my sorceress will raise a blackness shot with lightnings. She will cause it to sweep about the caravan. Your cut-purses will move with that black cloud, hidden behind it. Those with weapons will attack the guards. The weaponless men with us will snatch up those fallen weapons and join in the fighting."

The men muttered delightedly among themselves. "When the guards are dead, the looting will begin. All I ask is the magical properties on their way to Jokaline. No more. You and these men can have the gold, the silken stuffs, any jewels the caravan is carrying."

These men would follow him to Haderos and back, if he asked, Kyrik saw as he ran his stare around him. Even Almorak deferred to him.

The bearded chieftain said, "There is a caravan due today. It's a big one, far too big for me ever to have thought of attacking. It's due in another two hours, or about high noon."

"We'll be there. I'll go hurry Aryalla in her necromancy."

He found the woman crouched above a fire, whispering to the red and blue flames, to the yellow and the lavender tongues of fire that she caused by sprinkling ground herbs on the glowing coals. She did not raise her head as his shadow fell across her face but continued with her singsong ritual. When she was done, she sat back on her heels and raised her eyes to his face. She looked exhausted, Kyrik thought. "It is done. The blackness will come to the edge of the trees, and it will move as you direct."

Between the trees, that blackness was already gathering.

Chapter 7

The outlaws stared at that darkness, saw it shot through with streaks of vivid lightnings, red as the fires of Haderon. The ebon mist grew, it stretched now as far as they could see, between them and the road to Tantagol City. And Kyrik laughed, and his laughter was a booming note of triumph.

His big hand tightened on Aryalla. "You've done well, woman! By Illis, but you have. And you say that thing will obey me?"

She nodded, black eyes watching him. "Go before us," bellowed the barbarian. "But cling you to the ground, you clouds. I don't want to warn the caravan what will happen. Come, you others!"

He plunged between the trees, running easily. Yet more easily, the blackness and the lightnings went before him, slipping between the tree-boles and close to the little forest flowers clustering at their bases, not harming anyone, merely running as a sea-wave runs upon the shore.

"Kyrik! Jokaline will know Aryalla made magic!"

"Let him," he growled to the serpent voice. "The deed will be done by the time he can send soldiers."

Then the road was before them, broad and dusty, and they could hear the camel bells, for this caravan was from distant Arazalla, and the creaking of saddle leather, and the shouts of marching men. It came around a bend in that road and straightened ranks for the last long pull toward Tantagol City. Kyrik could see the painted wagons, the covered carts, the armed riders who cantered beside them. For almost a mile that vast cortege stretched, raising dust clouds that hovered over them and made men cough and spit to clear their throats.

The blackness lay curled at his feet, waiting. When the caravan was fully extended along the road so that he could see how long it was, Kyrik rose to his full height. His hand waved with Bluefang.

"At them," he told the blackness. "Take the men—but touch not the horses or the slave girls."

From the woodlands the black cloud poured like smoke, rising upward in the manner of a wave, and it fell upon the warriors and the merchants. The darkness was silent, its red lightnings made no sound. Yet now the man began to scream, and in their throats was the agony of tortured flesh. A few broke free, and Kyrik with the outlaws ran to meet them. His great sword swung, clove a rider half in two. Him, Kyrik jerked lifeless from the saddle, mounted in his place. He turned the horse, rode in upon the others, blued blade flashing in the sunlight.

Heavily armed and guarded was that caravan. Yet it was as nothing before the outlaws' swords and daggers, and the ebon mist that ate at living human flesh as if with the fanged mouths of a demon multitude. Dust rose upward into the air, men screamed and bellowed

Death is always silent. And death lay like a pall upon the crumpled cloaks and mail shirts of the caravan warriors, on the fallen silks of the merchants. For no flesh remained to them, it was gone as if picked clean by carrion birds. Only their bones remained, glistening whitely in the sun.

Kyrik stood in his stirrups. "Begone, black cloud of Aryalla! You have served me well this day. I will not forget!"

Slowly, as though the wind itself blew it away, the darkness shifted, lost color, its red lightnings faded out, and in wisps of the grayish smoke, it blew across the wild-wood and was gone. There remained only the outlaws and the screaming slave girls bound for the Tantagol marketplace, with Kyrik.

Almorak was at his elbow, "What now, Lord?" Kyrik grinned, "I'd give the women to your men, but I have a need for them, as you have for the armor and the trappings of the caravan warriors. Bid your men hide themselves also in the silken robes of the merchants—Illis knows they're big enough to hide them, armor and all—those merchants were so fat."

Aryalla came to the edge of the road, "What now?" she called.

"Jokaline will know you worked magic, you've got to ride with us. He'll be sending soldiers here to arrest and imprison any magicians who make magic in Tantagol unless they do it with his consent." Kyrik grinned, "Get in there with the slave girls. You'll be safe enough with them."

"And the families of the outlaws?"

"They'll hide in the haunted valley. They have nothing to fear, now that Isthinissis has been destroyed."

As Aryalla walked toward those painted wagons that held the female slaves, Kyrik saw around him the bustle of order coming out of chaos. The skeletons of dead men lined the roads. The outlaws, neatly clad in the armor and cloaks of the guards, sat their saddles, waiting for their marching orders. Kyrik lifted Bluefang high, pointed down the road. The caravan began to move.

Almorak came riding to join him at the point of the column, bluff in his leather coat with chain-mail shirt over it, a scarlet cloak thrown across his broad shoulders. He was big, not so huge as Kyrik, but the same confidence glowed in his eyes.

He said, "A quick attack on the palace, eh? We take Devadonides and slay him, and after him, his wizards?"

"Not so. The palace is set with traps. I go alone into it. You others—your outlaw band—shall guard the entrances, the exits. Let none pass in or out, and when the palace guard attacks, you fight them."

Almorak showed his teeth in a cold grin. "Fighting, aye. My lads will be for that And when we're done? When the palace guard no longer exists?"

"I shall have found Devadonides and Jokaline. I'll have won by that time—or lost."

Almorak cast a dubious eye at him. "What's this talk of losing?"

Kyrik growled, "I'm not worried about his fighting men. It's only his magicks I fear. And yet—I have certain powers of my own."

They rode on through the heat of the day and the dust and when the sun was beginning to sink westward, they came at last to the great gates of Tantagol City. The merchant banners were recognized by the guards, they waved hands and grinned and tried to catch glimpses of the slave girls where they sat or stood in the painted wagons.

To the market square went the caravan, and when they had taken up their places, Kyrik dismounted and walked to the wagons. Order was coming out of chaos, the outlaws were well trained, well disciplined.

"I'll need gifts for Devadonides," he told Almorak. "Two of the loveliest slave-girls, a coffer or two of gold, of precious gems. Then we ride to the palace."

With the slave-girls, he took Aryalla, still wearing the torn silken tunic that showed her body. They made a little cortege, with them walked the outlaws clad in expensive silks and velvet, as rich merchants. The palace guards grinned at sight of them, for Kyrik had a purse filled with golden griffs, which he scattered with a lavish hand. Most of the armed outlaws paused to talk with the guards while Kyrik with the false merchants passed through the stone doorway into the palace proper.

It had been a thousand years since he had walked these tiled floors, through these palace hallways, hung with old banners of victories long ago won on many fields of battle. There were also ancient weapons, the sword of his grandfather, of his father, left here as spoils of conquest by the first Devadonides. Only the rich draperies, the arrases of Invaren velvet, of Inisfalian silks, were new. A wide marbled staircase filled the foyer of this lower floor, led upward to the great keep that was the palace proper. It was in this keep with its thick stone walls, whispered the serpent voice in his mind, where Jokaline had his chambers, his necromantic rooms. There would Devadonides be, harking to his mage.

Guardsmen came to prevent them from leaving the staircase and moving onto the upper floor. They scorned the golden griffs Kyrik held out to them. They linked arms and fronted the barbarian with their mailed chests.

"None go above here except on order of King Devadonides," one said.

Kyrik sighed, stood to one side as Aryalla stepped forward. Her hand flashed, and brilliant globes of light lifted from her fingers, sped so swiftly toward the faces of the guardsmen they had no chance to ward them off. Like soap bubbles that children blow from clay pipes, they were; yet when they touched those hard, implacable faces, they burst and the guardsmen sank to the floor as in a coma.

Kyrik, Almorak and Aryalla stepped over them, moved onward, posting as staircase guards the outlaws in merchant's robes. These upper floors, Kyrik knew as he knew his name. Yet he knew also that there were magical traps set for them, traps which only Illis might discover. He drew Bluefang, held it up. And the serpent writhed, came to life. Its scaled head lifted, quested as though it sniffed for danger. Aryalla cried out in surprise, Almorak in awe as the serpent-being hissed softly.

"A stone yonder, that tilts on an iron axis! Kyrik went first, touched the edge of the stone with the tip of his blade. The flagstone pivoted, opened. Below, he could see a pit of alligators slithering here and there in a pool of fetid water.

"By the gods," growled Almorak. "Unwarned, we'd have stumbled into that place. Give me a good, clean death—not something like that."

They skirted the flagstone, moved on. The serpent was quivering, upright on the hilt of Bluefang. Its flat head darted here and there, its blue eyes blazed. "A mist, Kyrik! A mist hidden behind stone walls — ready to spew forth and envelop us all! Go warily, my lover. Wait for a moment until I—I—yes! That shadow on the wall . . . duck below it!"

They bent their heads, they crawled along the paving-stones until they were beyond the reach of that shadow band of power. Kyrik grinned coldly, resuming his normal height.

"Illis! Any fool who might blunder in here would be twice dead already! It's a good thing you're with us, demon-woman!"

The serpent hissed tenderly, wrapping its warmth about the hand that held the blade. Gently she rubbed her scaly head against his knuckles.

Aryalla muttered, "Faugh. In love with a snake. I might have known."

Illis reared, stared at the sorceress with glittering eyes. "Woman, I am Illis! Would you know my power?"

Aryalla shivered, moved closer to Almorak. Once more the she—snake upreared itself, stared along the corridor where they must walk. "There is no danger here. Not until. . ."

They moved on, walking warily despite the assurance of the snake-woman Now they came to a narrow staircase, and paused. Kyrik put a foot on a stone tread, moved upward. The others followed.

His animal instincts were aroused, now, sharpened by the dangers they had passed. His hand took a firmer grip on Bluefang, he moved it ahead of him, wanting to know if any other magicks were at work. And the serpent-being on that hilt quested also, snake-head darting back and forth. It was Kyrik who halted suddenly, eyes lifted to the angled ceiling high above. And Illis asked, "What is it, lover?"

"That shadow on the ceiling. That's not a natural thing; it wasn't there when I ruled in this palace."

"There is no magic!" Kyrik thrust his sword forward at arm's length, stepped up a tread and two. His bull voice roared, "Back, you others!" And from above a great stone square came hurtling downward.

It almost caught the barbarian, only his animal instincts saved him by a backward leap. His body caught Aryalla and Almorak, sent them tumbling heels over head down the staircase. They brought up in a heap at its base, staring upward.

The stone was near enough to touch. Kyrik put out a hand, ran his fingers over the stone block. The stone was quivering against his flesh.

"I sensed it not, Kyrik!"

"Na, na. This was no magic. It was simply a trap set by human means, on a spring that the movement of my sword set off. Sly Devadonides. He trusts neither to magic nor to non-magic, alone. His traps are of every kind."

Kyrik turned, gestured Aryalla and Almorak to follow. They climbed over the stone block that would have crushed the barbarian like an ant under a heel, had it landed. They went even more cautiously, with Kyrik adding his green eyes to those of the serpent-woman as each scanned treads and walls and ceiling for further danger. They came to the upper floor, and now they could hear the sonorous voice of a man evoking help from a demon. Illis hissed, "You must hurry, Kyrik. Haste must be your guardian, now. Jokaline calls on—Absothoth!"

Kyrik knew the name and power of that dread being. Absothoth lived in the nether worlds of Absora and Absoron, he was baleful, malignant. Hate was in his heart, his head, and he obeyed only those who fed his life with human blood. His hand tightened on Bluefang as he leaped forward.

To Haderos with danger. If it came, well and good. If it did not, he would be inside that magical chamber where Jokaline summoned up the evil demons who waited on his call. His war-boots skimmed the floor, ahead were two bronze doors. Tightly barred, he reasoned. He left his feet in a long leap, thudded into those bronze barriers. The sound of his crash against that metal resounded like the strokes of a gong struck with an iron hammer, up and down the hall where Aryalla and Almorak came hurrying. The blow was titanic, Kyrik bounced off that metal as though it had pushed him. On one knee, he studied those doors, scowling.

Illis whispered, "Let me handle them, Kyrik." And now her voice rose in a singsong wail, almost too shrill for the ears of humans to hear. A ringing cry answered the first few notes of that song, and Kyrik heard a man curse. Then the doors were opening. Kyrik leaped forward. Something small and leathery swooped at him from the air above. The barbarian had a glimpse of a great red pentagram, a smaller pentagram, each with a man crouched inside them. One was Jokaline, tall and sinister, with a long white beard and long white hair under a pointed cap. The other was a small, plump man, with moon-face and tiny eyes half hidden under rolls of fat. Jokaline—and Devadonides, the king. And set between the two pentagrams was a great crystal prism.

Kyrik whirled, lifted a hand. He tried to stab that leathery thing with his sword, but he was too slow, too late. Its fanged jaws opened to close on his arm. Inside him, Kyrik knew that once those yellowed fangs drew his blood, he would die in the agonies of a poisoned death.

Aye! Swift was that bat-like entity, swooping low. But—swifter even than it, was Illis. The snake darted outward, keeping contact with the sword Kyrik held only by its tail as its own mouth opened, darted and closed on leathery flesh. The bat-thing howled in agony, fluttered against the fangs that held it, beating at that snake-head with its wings.

Eyes closed, the snake held on. And the leathery thing died, falling to the ground as the snake-woman opened her mouth. Kyrik shook himself from a momentary paralysis, sprang forward.

Toward the greater pentagram he hurled himself, toward Jokaline. The old man screeched, shouted indistinguishable words. The great prism set into the floor darkened, grew black, shot through with green flames.

"Absothoth comes," whispered Illis. Kyrik was inside the pentagram, had caught the old man in a mighty hand, whirled him upward off his feet, hurled him. Through the air he flung him, right at that great prism. His old body hit the crystal facets of the living gem, collapsed at its base as he slid down those smooth, hard sides.

And Kyrik turned toward Devadonides. The fat little man was crouched in his kingly robes, quivering with fright. His eyes bulged, his mottled jowls shook in the ague of terror that held him in his grasp.

"Stay away, stay away I am the king!"

Kyrik barked laughter. "A king? You? Pah, you disgust me. No king are you, Devadonides—but an usurper. I am the king of Tantagol. I am—Kyrik of the Victories!"

He leaped from the larger pentagram into the smaller. The king scuttled backward to the edge of the design. His face was ashen, he shook as does the aspen in the grip of an autumn gale.

"Kyrik? Kyrik of the—Victories?" he croaked. "That Kyrik is dust, long centuries gone. My forefather slew him."

"Na, na, little man. Your father was no more courageous than you. He had a spell put on me, turned me into a statue. I lived. I thought. I told myself that one day I would have vengeance."

Illis screamed. Kyrik whirled. The prism was melting, flowing into nothingness. And from its deep a dark being was rising upward, amorphous, evil, its fangs showing in a triumphant grin. What served for its eyes—red stars that glittered with demonic fury—glanced down at the gibbering Jokaline who sought to crawl from the base of the great prism that was its doorway into this world, away from that which he had summoned. Outside the great pentagram Jokaline was prey to that which had served him and obeyed his commands across the many years. Well he knew that hatred Absothoth held for him and so he tried to flee.

"Great Absothoth. Mighty lord of the nether hells! Always I have worshiped you. Always have I given sacrifice in your name. Living men, living women, all have been fed to you—by me!"

The black being laughed, booming laughter that rang in the chamber. "Only by that sacrifice could you command me, Jokaline. You gave me helpless humans to further your own ends, to keep me in thrall to you. Now—I find you outside the pentagram !"

Something like a black hand, a clawed paw, darted. It sank into Jokaline, held him motionless as a quivering mouse is motionless under the paws of a cat. The star-like eyes went around the chamber.

"I see Devadonides, in whose name you called me."

The little man hurled himself at Kyrik's feet, clasped his brawny legs. "Save me from it. Don't throw me to that thing the way you did Jokaline. Save me, and anything in my kingdom belongs to you.

"Na, na. You have no kingdom. Not any longer. Tantagol is mine. It belongs to Kyrik of the Victories. As once it did, long and long ago."

Booming laughter rose upward. "Fools You all belong to me, all of you.

"Jokaline—the only one among you who might have commanded my obedience—is out of the pentagram and helpless. And you others—pahh! You are as nothing to Absothoth. As motes of sand in a desert. Yet you live—and while you live, I am not pleased. And so. . ."

The blackness surged forward. A woman screamed.

Aryalla, thought Kyrik, swinging Bluefang at the blackness, striving to reach the glowing red green flames in that ebon being with his point. She would be swept up by Absothoth, carried with him and the others into his nether hells. As would he, himself. The blackness was closing on him, he could feel it like clinging wetness all about him—evil, evil Rapacious and greedy for human life, for the blood of living men and women.

"Illis!" he bellowed, struggling. The snake-woman was silent. Borne off his feet—he collided with Almorak and Aryalla as they were drawn toward the giant gem he toppled sideways, not daring to use Bluefang any longer, fearful of slicing its edges into human flesh. He waited like a trapped animal, patient and unmoving, no longer fighting the whipping folds of the blackness devouring him, drawing him toward the huge gem and into it, into glittering prisms of light and color.

Downward, downward, ever downward. . . . . Winds howled. Coldness numbed his flesh. Heat seared his bones. His head pounded with pain and his mouth opened to cry out in agony. Was he being devoured alive? Could this be—death?

Then his war-boots hit solid ground and he stood erect, Bluefang still in his right hand, with the serpent twined about his wrist. Illis was warm, alive, thank her tinted toenails. His eyelids unlocked and he stared around him.

He saw a barren land, of gray rocks and gray dirt, and a wind blowing, far away, where dust crawled across the landscape. The sky was gray, with no clouds, with no familiar blueness in it. And the cold He shivered, stamped his feet. He could see a long way across this flat land. Here and there was a broken pillar, a tumbled—in dwelling—a temple of some sort?—and a few scattered shards of masonry. There was no sign of Absothoth. In this world he ruled, he might not be a black cloud, Kyrik knew. He might be—anything. The barbarian rumbled fury in his throat at sight of Jokaline, even now staggering to his feet, and fat Devadonides, lying prone on the cold ground.

"At least, I can slay you both," he growled. "No, Kyrik. They must live!" His mind questioned, but Illis would not answer. The demon woman had her own reasons for saving the mage and the king; their being alive would serve his purpose best, and so he turned to Aryalla, who was leaning against Almorak, seeking warmth from her nearness to his big body.

"Well, sorceress? Can you get us out of here?" Aryalla pushed away from the outlaw chieftain, ran her eyes around the bare rocks and barren land. She shivered.

"I have not my coffer, my magical materials." Kyrik grinned at her. "I told you I could never fully succeed in my quest for the throne of Tantagol, when we started out on this quest. This is where it ends, here in this dead world." He scowled. "We're here like pigs in a pen, waiting for Absothoth to feed on us at his leisure."

"Not—quite, Kyrik!"

"Now what will you mean, Illis of the blue eyes?"

I—wait. Soon will Absothoth come in his real guise. Ahh, and only then can I attack him. Only then will my own godhood fully touch his own."

The wind grew colder. It whistled across these gray waters and Devadonides wept, huddled in his garments. "I was a fool to listen to you," he said to Jokaline, who stood with head bowed, white beard and hair flying. "You counseled me to ask for Absothoth, you said he would have to obey." The little pig eyes looked at Kyrik. "You said none could come at me, safe in the protection of your spells. Yet that barbarian walked through...the traps you set."

Jokaline stirred. "Not by wit alone. There was magic involved. The girl?" He stared at Aryalla. "Was it her spells that passed them by the shadow band, the reptile pit? I—know not."

The serpent quivered against Kyrik's hand. "There is other danger, Kyrik Danger—I sense! Yet I cannot act on it. It threatens us all. Not as Absothoth threatens, but in some other way. A way I cannot guard against!"

Kyrik growled low in his throat. His hand touched the hilt of his sword, fell away. What need of a sword here, where none could do him harm? Jokaline was an old man, Devadonides but a bundle of whimpering flesh that bore him no more danger than might a plump pudding.

They walked about, Kyrik taking Aryalla and Almorak with him, studying the gray landscape, the rocks and the very ground. From time to time he growled low in his throat, he lacked an enemy to fight.

"Somewhere, there is an answer," he told them at last.

Aryalla stared at him. "What answer?"

"You're a sorceress, alive to these things. You say you studied with your father, Gorsifal. From a very child, you studied magicks. Can't you think of something that will get us out of this place?"

"It's the realm of Absothoth. Something links us to it. Yes, this much I know. What that something is, I know not."

"Think, then," he snapped. "Our lives depend on you."

Almorak said, "Give me an enemy I can see, can fight. This land—bah! It's dead. There isn't a bird in the sky, not even a lizard crawling along the ground.

"And without an enemy to strike at, our swords are useless," nodded Kyrik. "Still, there must be a way. . . . . ?"

He stood with bent head; he himself was a warlock. He had made magicks long and long ago, in Tantagol City, for this gift of necromancy he had inherited from his ancestors who had been wizards as well as warriors. He waited, patient as the cat, for some sign, some rhythm out of line with nature, which might afford him the clue he needed to act.

Illis too, quested. He could feel the stabbings of her spirit, the curiosity which was a palpable thing in his mind. She went this way and that with her keen brain, seeking that which she would know and recognize as the link between them and Absothoth which must be severed if they hoped to stay alive.

And then Devadonides screamed. They whirled, they saw him flapping his robes as though he were a giant bat caught by its claws on the ground and trying to fly upward. They saw the stark terror on his fat face, the protruding eyes, the contorted mouth. His arms he waved as if they might carry him away from that which held him. Aryalla screamed.

"Illis," breathed Kyrik. "I hear, I see, lover Ansothoth—feeds!" From side to side, Devadonides twisted, but his feet remained in the same place. And now Kyrik felt the skin crawl upon his neck and back, for he could see, where his royal robes flapped back, that Devadonides' feet were implanted on the ground and seemed to be—melting.

Aye! The flesh ran like molten wax down to the gray rock and the rock sucked at his flesh, his blood, and Devadonides shrank a little at every moment. He was not big to begin with, he was mostly fat, he could offer little opposition to that which held him in its grip. His mouth was open: he howled in abysmal fear.

Kyrik snarled, yanked Bluefang out, sprang forward. Jokaline shrank back, staring from Devadonides to the leaping barbarian in fright that matched that of the king.

"I cannot tell what it is, Kyrik! Kyrik slid to a halt before the plump little man. He stared at him from head to toe. He saw nothing that was causing this except the ground itself. And so he drove the point of Bluefang into the dirt, stabbing again and again.

Laughter boomed down from the sky. "Fool. Think you to deprive Absothoth of his just reward? Long have I hungered for the blood and flesh of this stupid little thing, who used Jokaline to order me to help him commit his sins. My power fed his greed, his lusts. Without me and Isthinissis, he would have been nothing Well, Isthinissis is dead. Slain by you, barbarian. But you can never kill me. For here, I am the world itself. Aye, I am the ground you stand on, which will drink your blood, your flesh—next And there is nothing you can do about it."

Kyrik quivered with the helplessness that ran in him with his blood. "Give me a foe. A dozen foes to strike down with my sword. This way—I am nothing!"

With a grim snarl he lifted Bluefang and drove it at Devadonides. "At least, I can deprive Absothoth of the life he craves—must have."

"No, Kyrik There is—another way! Illis' scream rang in his mind as he slid to a halt.

Chapter 8

Understanding burst in Kyrik. He needed not the hissed cry that was the goddess to tell him where to place his blued blade. He was warlock, he was warrior. Intuitively, it came to him. And yet Illis spoke to him, counseled him.

"Jokaline is the link His necromancies summoned Absothoth up from this gray world, his magical energies kept him slave to his command. Destroy Jokaline and snap the thread. Destroy Jokaline. Jokaline! Jokaline!"

Kyrik whirled sideways and dove. The necromancer screamed, whirled to run. If Kyrik needed proof of his decision, he had it before him in the long, skinny legs of the mage, his flapping robes and pumping arms. Jokaline knew!

"Touch not your feet to the ground more than you can help, lover! Already Absothoth abandons Devadonides, turns on you. Once he grips you with his suckers, you won't be able to move!

That voice was as a scream in his brain. And Kyrik felt the nippings of tiny teeth at his war-boots as he ran. In another moment or two the ground would catch him, melt his flesh and his bones, drain him of his blood. Kyrik stumbled. To fall meant certain death.

And then Kyrik called upon his battle skills. Back went his arm. Forward it shot. His fingers loosed their grip and Bluefang sped through the air as might a steel arrow, straight for the back of the running magician. Time hung suspended for the barbarian. He saw the racing necromancer, the speeding sword. His own feet stumbled, felt the nippings of tiny teeth, staggered.

His sword went into Jokaline. From backbone through his chest and out in front of him, went that blued steel blade-red now, where it thrust from his rib-cage, dripping blood—and Jokaline cried out with the terror of death inside him. He fell forward, dying. . .

Blackness swirled about Kyrik. He woke to the sound of a woman screaming, opened blurred eyes to see the gypsy girl, Myrnis, springing after Kangor who was the commander of the palace guards. A dagger glittered in the gypsy's hand. Kyrik saw dimly the faint, blurry outlines of Jokaline's necromantic chamber.

Kangor laughed and sprang away from Myrnis toward the glass prism. His sword was raised on high. "I'll keep them all in that land where Absothoth rules," he bellowed. .

Kyrik sought to move to stop him, but could not. Myrnis leaped. Her dagger flashed in the candlelight. To the hilt she buried that blade inside Kangor. And the guards commander screeched, head thrown back, feet missing their steps so that he fell forward and lay upon the prism for a long moment. Then he slid down its faceted surface as had Jokaline, but when he touched the floor, he was dead.

Myrnis stared around her, panting. Blood dripped from her dagger. And Kyrik found the blackness leaving him, saw the outline of the magic chamber solidify, grow strong. He rested on his side, staring. All about him, as if out of the mists, the others were appearing. Aryalla, Almorak, the dead body of Devadonides, badly shrunken, and that of Jokaline, still with Bluefang in him, were now in the chamber with him. Myrnis cried out at sight of the barbarian, ran to him. "Kyrik! By the gods, I was right. We were leaving Tantagol City when you came into it with your outlaws. I saw you, recognized you. I brought Romanoy fighting men with me to side those outlaws who were forced to fight Devodonides' guards."

Her brown hands pulled him to his feet. He asked, "There was a battle?" She hooted, "Not much of a one. The outlaws and my gypsies fought like fiends, they were battling for freedom and the overthrow of Devadonides. They cut down the guards until they surrendered—and all that was left of them—except for Kangor who turned and fled, with me on his heels."

Myrnis turned, pointed at the prism. "He would have shattered that!"

"And kept us penned in that blackness between the magical and the ordinary worlds," whispered Aryalla, ashen of face and trembling, moving toward them with Almorak to support her. "There, we would have floated, drifted for all eternity. . ."

She sobbed. Myrnis smiled gently, nodding. Kyrik growled, putting a hand on the gypsy girl. "Aye, he would have made himself ruler of Tantagol, I think. He must have watched from some hidden place, seen all that took place. He went to lead his men in the fight, then when he knew that battle lost, came here to keep us—where we were!"

Almorak rumbled, "What of that carrion?" His hand indicated the body of dead Devadonides. Kyrik chuckled. "We'll give him a royal funeral, by the gods. We'll bury him with his forefathers. I want no question about his being alive, to stir up men to rebel against my rule in Tantagol."

Aryalla glanced at him, lips curving into a smile. "Then you will be its king?"

"In name only, girl. Not for me the throne with its invisible bands to chain a man to duty." His green eyes studied the sorceress. "You shall be my regents, you and Almorak. How like you that, outlaw? Regent of Tantagol City!"

Almorak, grinned, then scowled. "I'd be a bad regent, Kyrik. I'd cut taxes, I'd repeal all outlawry, I'd think of my people first, myself last."

Kyrik nodded grimly. "And so say I You have permission to do all these things, for it's what I intended doing myself, if ever I did become king again. No more wars of conquest. Only—peace!"

Myrnis asked slyly, "And what will you be doing, King Kyrik?"

He grinned down at her, finding her appealing in her torn skirt, the sheer blouse and leather bodice. His arm went around her yielding middle, drawing her to him.

"You Romanoys travel across the world. I may go with you, to see it." He drew a deep breath, eyes bright. "I've been a long time dead. I want to see the changes that Time has made in my world. I want to drink deep of ale in strange taverns, fight men I've never met, sample foods from Arazalla to northern Arborea. In short, I want to live."

Aryalla said quietly, "You have a duty to your people."

"Not I. You wanted vengeance, woman. There's your revenge."

His finger pointed at the thing that had been King Devadonides. Aryalla stared, nodding. From the body to the chamber her eyes moved. "This place shall be boarded up. Closed as long as I'm co-regent with Almorak."

The outlaw had been studying Kyrik. "Aren't you afraid Aryalla and I may usurp your kingship? By the gods! I'd never trust any man I've only known for such a little while to sit on my throne. Nor woman, either."

Kyrik shrugged. "I never sought the throne. I only promised to overthrow Devadonides." He brooded at the dead king. "May-hap someday I'll want to rule. But not now, not for a long time. You two shall sit in my place."

He showed his teeth in a cold grin. "As long as you rule well, that is. By Illis! Kingship corrupts a man. Its power goes to his head. Don't let it go to yours. Or I'll come back to take it away from you."

He put an arm about Myrnis. "Come, girl. I want food and drink, and a few of your sweet-lipped kisses."

Aryalla protested, "What about the dead king?" Kyrik sighed. "Aye! I do have a duty, after all. I must bring order, here in Tantagol, first—before I can go wandering. Let's to the guards, below."

He yanked Bluefang out of Jokaline, cleaned and sheathed it, feeling the warmth of Illis—snake against his hand. They went out of the necromantic chamber, Kyrik in the lead. Down the staircase to the outlaws and the sullen guards they went, and here Kyrik paused to eye the disarmed men.

"I rule in Tantagol now," he told them. "Devadonides is dead—slain by Absothoth himself. My name is Kyrik of the Victories."

Their eyes lighted up, studying him. These men were warriors, they recognized in him a warrior greater than they, a king to whom it would be an honor to dip a knee or bend a head.

"You can wear my livery—or you can leave Tantagol. I offer you your lives and the choice. Kangor too is dead, and this man, this Almorak, will be coregent and your commander from now on."

A big man with a scar on his cheek growled, "We like your terms, Kyrik. We are your men."

He went with his guard about him out into the city streets. There were people here, staring and worried, and Kyrik went among them to take their hands and speak with them, promising a lessening of their taxes, an easing of their lives. There would be no more torturers; if a man committed a crime and deserved to die so that the rest of society would be safe, then it would be clean, swift death.

Through the night he went, into the taverns and the alehouses, and spoke with the common man and his woman, and left them with tears in their eyes.

Peace and contentment was come upon all Tantagol, he assured them, there would be a celebration at his expense when men could feast and become drunk and make love, and there would be no curfew, nor any spies to stare upon them and report their words.

Myrnis walked with him all the way, swaggering a little. From time to time her brown eyes assessed the bulk of the barbarian, soft and tender in their regard. She would touch him with her hand as she stood beside him, or brush his hip with hers as they walked the cobblestoned streets.

And when the two moons began to sink beyond the city spires, it was Myrnis who turned and strode with him back toward the palace, for there Kyrik would sleep this night in evidence of his kingship, and Myrnis meant to sleep beside him. His arm was about her waist, holding her close, his head was bent to stare down into her eyes.

Thus it was that Kyrik did not see the pulsing light that framed itself against the windows of his palace for a brief moment—and was gone.

They came into the palace, guards saluted. Up the staircase to the bedroom which was now his by right of kingship, came Kyrik of the Victories. Servants had changed the bedding, had replaced the livery of King Devadonides with his own gold dragon on a black field. He noted these things only vaguely, for he was more interested in the breasts of Myrnis which he could see half revealed by her blouse, pushed up by her laced leather bodice, and in the sway of her hips and the stridings of her shapely bare legs.

As he unstrapped his sword-belt, Kyrik touched his eyes to the golden snake entwined about the hilt.

Illis had not spoken to his mind in a long time. Yet she was still within the snake, and a sense of uneasiness touched Kyrik.

But Myrnis was undoing her bodice lacings and her breasts were pushing out at him, so he forgot Illis and his momentary worry, and grinned, stripping of his habergeon, his war-boots and his gambeson. Naked they met in the middle of the room, kissed. Kyrik picked up the gypsy girl, carried her to the huge bed. He fell on her, was clasped in turn...

Dawn was in the air when Illis whispered to his mind, rousing him from satiated slumber. Kyrik turned, groaning. Myrnis was a weight upon his chest, his arm tightened about her sleeping body.

"Go away, Illis. I've worshiped to you all through what was left of the night. Let me sleep."

"Sluggard! Death creeps on you!" Kyrik opened blurry eyes. Tiredness fell from him like a garment, for well he knew the goddess spoke not idly, at any time. Myrnis stirred, moaned a protest.

"Ignore the girl, fool Kyrik–or you die!" He came out of bed as Myrnis protested sleepily. Naked he stood on the carpeted floor, and his hand went to the serpent hilt of Bluefang.

"What is it? Who brings death to Kyrik?"

"Absothoth comes!"

"Absothoth? But that demon's back in his gray world. He can't harm me. Why should he?"

"Why should he? You cheated him of Jokaline. It was Jokaline he wanted, most of all. First Devadonides, then Almorak and Aryalla. Then you. This was to have been the manner of their dying. You he would save, then take just before he did!

Jokaline, except that I told you Jokaline was the bond keeping us in that world. And when you attacked the old mage, Absothoth had to slay you."

"And did not."

"He comes now, Kyrik And—nothing can stop him."

There were tears in Illis' voice. Already she sorrowed for her lover. Kyrik felt a vast anger. "Is there any way to slay him?"

"Nay. None!"

Myrnis was sitting up in bed, naked as Kyrik. Her eyes were big, her slightly swollen lips open. "Why stand you there, lover?"

His green eyes touched her softness. Kyrik grinned, swung aside, moved to a palace window. He pushed it open, felt the cool night air.

"Myrnis, come to me." She sprang from the rumpled bed-coverings, ran naked to his side, eyes questioning. But before she could speak, she sniffed and made a face.

"That stench, Kyrik! What is it?"

"Absothoth," he breathed. "He comes for me." Myrnis shuddered, crept into his arm. "Then we'll die together. I don't want to live, without you."

"I'm not dead yet," he growled. The fetid odor was stronger now, and they could hear the faint slither of something in the dark hall beyond the closed door of the bedchamber. His hand was tight about Bluefang's hilt, his every muscle quivered. The demon god was coming. He had fled from that gray land which was himself, had come into Kyrik's world after him, seeking his own vengeance.

His eyes stared through the gathering dawn that lighted the room. He saw the big oak door, saw also that which was beyond it, seeping in through the crack between floor and door. A black slime, sliding, spreading...

Myrnis screamed. Her flesh jammed against that of Kyrik, she turned her head and buried her face against his chest. "Kill it, Kyrik—kill it."

"Illis says no man can kill that thing." The black slime spread, came across the carpet for them. Kyrik sensed the malevolence of the thing, it was proud and its pride demanded that he who had robbed him of his vengeance on Jokaline must die, must be absorbed by this slime that was his essence.

And still Kyrik waited. Not until the ebon ooze was a yard from his bare foot and Myrnis had fainted in his arms did he turn and fling himself at the open window. Naked he went out into the dawn and his hands and toes sought holes in the worn stone ornaments of the palace wall. Myrnis lay across a shoulder, inert. He did not feel her weight as he began his climb.

Upward he went, always upward, until the lead tiles of the roof were just above him. He pulled himself up, ran along the tiles until he came to a narrow door that opened to one side of a stone chimney. "What are you doing?" Illis asked his brain. "There's only one way to stop that thing. Destroy the prism between its world and ours, as Kangor would have done if Myrnis hadn't killed him!"

"Absothoth knows. He speeds, now."

"Then it becomes a race between us." He flung open the narrow door, ran down the stone steps. This was part of that labyrinthine way that twined and twisted between the palace rooms, all the way down into the ancient dungeons. As a boy he had played in these hidden corridors, spied upon the servants; he knew them as he knew his face.

Down those treads three at a time he ran, one arm holding Myrnis to him, his right hand gripping Bluefang. He opened a door, stepped into the necromantic chamber. Already it had been boarded up, he could see the nails that Almorak had ordered the palace carpenters to place there.

The doors would not stop Absothoth, who could flow under and around them. The blackness would be in the room, very soon. There would be no time, then, even to think. He must act now.

The black slime poured over and under the barred door, its odor nauseating. Kyrik sprang, blued blade raised high.

Sprang also—Absothoth—The demon god shaped itself into a monstrous humanoid with long arms, with demon flames burning where its eyes should have been, and it lunged for the barbarian. He was too far from the prism. Absothoth would reach it first—

"It seeks only to escape! Let it go!"

"Never," bellowed the barbarian—and struck. Downward flashed that blued blade, through the ebon darkness it clove a path. Through its humanoid shape to the very prism went his sword. And its steel rang on that crystal, rang and rang. . . . .

A thousand arpeggios of crystalline tinklings answered that shattering touch of steel on faceted crystal. A pizzicato of unearthly sibilances beat against his ears. Magic was dying here with the demon-god, and both offered up their death cries as one, blending into carillons of agony, of bleak despair, of essences beyond human comprehension, utterly destroyed. Those chimings were everywhere about him, slamming against him, buffeting. He reeled and swayed.

And Illis—screamed! There was the death note in her voice. Kyrik froze, weeping inside himself. Had he killed the goddess who loved him, who protected and sheltered him? This he could not believe, and yet—

The blackness was gone. The crystal prism lay shattered. And Bluefang was in his right hand. Myrnis still lay unconscious on the floor. Ah, but the golden snake—lay limp also, beside a shard of broken prism.

Kyrik whispered, "Illis! Speak to me!" His hands raised the snake, held it. Slowly that serpentine form changed, altered, shimmering in the dawn-light flooding into the necromantic chamber. Dimly, Kyrik sensed what had happened. Only by her own powers, by her intervention, could he have slain that which was Absothoth. And Illis had offered her strength to his blade, had caused it to shear through non-flesh and into the crystal prism.

The snake was gone. Illis lay naked in his arms, broken, lifeless. Kyrik wept, silently. Slowly he turned away, leaving that chamber and the living woman inside it, to carry the dead woman down the stairs of the hidden way, to the altered room where he had placed the Luststone.

Tenderly he placed her on the altar, ran his eyes over her golden hair, the pearly flesh of her body. He knelt before that altar and that body a long time, grieving.

Would Illis ever come to him again? She had given her life for him. Or perhaps—only her demonic energies, which had caused her to flee back into that realm from which she had always come to aid him. At this thought, Kyrik raised his head, smiled.

"I shall wait," he told her cadaver. "Someday, you'll return to me."

He turned then and went up to the chamber where Myrnis was stirring and her he carried through the secret passageway and back to his bedchamber. She was murmuring now, and he reassured her, telling her that the danger was over, there was nothing more to fear. He placed her in the bed, sat beside her.

"We'll be away tomorrow for the wild-wood," he growled. "Let Aryalla and Almorak have Tantagol, I want it not." With a faint smile, he looked at her. "And you, girl? I saw the way you clung to me when we walked the city streets this night. Would you rather stay here in the city and rule a country as my queen?"

"It would be nice to be a queen," she said wistfully.

"You'll be my queen. Isn't that enough?" Myrnis smiled and nodded, putting her arms about him and drawing his lips down to the kisses of her mouth. Outside the open window, a bird was caroling.

END

Thank you for purchasing Gardner Francis Fox's Sword & Sorcery classic: Kyrik: Warrior Warlock.

Find out more about Mr. Fox by visiting

GARDNERFFOX.com

Manufactured by Amazon.ca
Acheson, AB